NOWHERENESS
IN THE WORLD

NOWHERENESS IN THE WORLD

DEJAN STOJANOVIĆ

Translated by
Željko Mitić

New Avenue Books

&

ALBATROS PLUS

NOWHERENESS IN THE WORLD
English translation Copyright © 2024 New Avenue Books

Nowhereness in the World is the English translation of the third book in the pentalogy titled *The World in Nowhereness*, originally written in Serbian. Although the third book shares the same title as the entire pentalogy, this edition uses *Nowhereness in the World* (Serbian: *Nigdina u svetu*), the title of the second part of the third book, to avoid any potential confusion. (Serbian: *Svet u nigdini* and a subtitle Pentalogija: *Ozar, Svet i Bog, Svet u nigdini, Svet i ljudi, Dom svetlosti.*)

New Avenue Books
&
Albatros Plus

First Edition in English

Library of Congress Control Number: 2024950755

ISBN-13: 979-8-9916352-7-1

THEY SAID ABOUT *THE WORLD IN NOWHERENESS*

"When I got my hands on Dejan Stojanović's book *The World in Nowhereness*, I was amazed and read the book with great pleasure. I did not even believe there was someone today who could write such a long poem, an epic, as if I opened to read the *Iliad* in our time. I recommend this book to all believers in poetry because faith in poetry is the same as faith in eternity and eternal life."

— *Matija Bećković*

"*The World in Nowhereness* is Dejan Stojanović's utopian absolute book, a Mallarméan absolute. An absolute story, or an absolute book, according to Borges, is a desert-like book: sandy, grainily unforeseeable, and corpuscularly innumerable. It is simultaneously a vision and a chimera. Isn't that precisely why we long for an absolute book? *The World in Nowhereness* by Dejan Stojanović is, in his way, an embodiment of that dream."

— *Srba Ignjatović*

"I have always wondered, even about my poetic work, what a total poem is… Can the pentalogy by Dejan Stojanović be called a total poem that every poet of note has dreamed about since Homer? I felt such impulses while reading *The World in Nowhereness*. This is an absolute poem, of an absolute system of thought that reaches across the totality of our civilizational legacies."

— *Duško Novaković*

"Exactly 17 years ago, in the last year of the 20th century, I came across the work of Dejan Stojanović, and then I wrote a text from which I will extract a few sentences. "Dejan Stojanović, in the last two years, made a real feat; he published six books, except for one, all books of poetry." This first five-book collection was published in the last year of the 20th century, and here we are now with the five-book collection in the XXI century, nearing the end of the second decade. And then I also wrote the following: "Stojanović is a poet who searches for the perfect poetic form because at the same time he searches for the absolute meaning of human existence." Whether it was a hunch or not, there is the Pentalogy, and there is that word, that concept – an absolute, an absolute book, an absolute poem that could be sensed even in that first pentalogy, in those poems that he published at that time."

— *Aleksandar Petrov* (January 17, 2018)

"(*The World in Nowhereness* offers) the joy of cognition due to discoveries worthy of the Nobel Prize…"

— *Milan Lukić*

"*The World in Nowhereness* is primarily the result of great literary ambition and faith in literature. It was not only Kiš who said that literature is created by form and that Sartre's quote should be placed at the entrance to the Association of Serbian Writers that "someone does not become a writer to say certain things, but to say them in a certain way." Dejan Stojanović is one of those who think well about that way and think very sovereignly and broadly. Even in how he approaches the form, we can see the breadth of his education, including the humanities and the natural sciences. However, perhaps more than anything else, he enters into some area of spirituality and, I would even dare say, esoteric. If you read Dejan Stojanović, your life will not be the same – it will be better."

— *Muharem Bazdulj*

"It has been quite a while since we had, if at all, a poetic pentalogy in Serbian poetry."

— *Dušan Stojković*

Dejan Stojanović's poetic-philosophical book *The World in Nowhereness*, both in form and content, is an original and exceptional literary work and can be considered a rare literary event in Serbian poetry and on the world stage.

— *Nevena Vitošević*

"It is every poet's dream to write a relevant, unique, comprehensive book in which he will properly present all his thoughts and feelings that have appeared in his long conversations with the world. By the *world,* I mean everything manifested and abstract in (a) language, what is named, and what can be named. Dejan Stojanović's extensive pentalogy *The World in Nowhereness* is an attempt at writing such a book. This pentalogy about the world and light is an ambitious endeavor."

— Bratislav R. Milanović

"*The World in Nowhereness*, the pentalogy by Dejan Stojanović, is an unusual endeavor in Serbian literature."

— Nikola Marinković

"*The World in Nowhereness*, a poetic endeavor by Dejan Stojanović, is an exceptional occurrence in Serbian."

— Dragan Kolarević

"There are very few such books in Serbian literature."

— Ivan Cvetanović

"(The publishing of *The World in Nowhereness* is) a significant date in contemporary Serbian poetry."

— Miljurko Vukadinović

"Steadfast and consistent, with his mapping out of circular trajectories in the realms of poetry and philosophy, and always being something more than the sum of all parts, Dejan Stojanović has proved to be a thinker of continuously inventive thought. He belongs to that creative ilk whose body of work affirms the permanence of the long-established unity of the Mystic and the Magus. On the one hand, he is one of those with extensive knowledge and who, according to Bela Hamvash, are Mystics. Yet, he is also one of the Magi, who also possesses knowledge, but one meant to encourage and reflect the urge to peer into the other, lesser-known or completely unexplored side, which light cannot reach at first glance."

— David Kecman Dako

Dejan Stojanović, a sincere devotee of both poetry and philosophy, achieved a real poetic feat in 2017 by publishing an extensive five-volume book titled *The World in Nowhereness*.

— Aleksandar B. Laković

"The author is deeply immersed in his attempt to decode the essence of the universe, the meaning of the origin, and the persistence of being therein. He seeks balance and the possibility of introducing harmony into seemingly incompatible, disharmonious phenomena and concepts."

— *Gordana Vlahović*

"Dejan Stojanović offers us *The World in Nowhereness*, his latest book, as a spiritual anthology. This is an ambitious poetic and essayistic project in a predominantly philosophical, dense, and layered pentalogy about humanity as the source and the final destination of all visible and invisible worlds. The manuscript is presented in innovative, avant-garde form. Dejan Stojanović wisely and expertly intertwines poetry and prose, the epic and the lyrical, and the theoretical-critical."

— *Zorica Arsić Mandarić*

"Stojanović's pronounced contemplativeness is what makes him stand out in the contemporary world of the poetic invention as one of the few being in no quandary about the equality of poetry and philosophy and the necessity of their proper understanding, as well as a deeper decoding of the meaning behind words. For that reason, I see his search in the book *The World in Nowhereness* as a quest for the meaning of elemental survival in a time that is alienated, brutally real, and preoccupied with everything and nothing."

— *Vidak Maslovarić*

"Stojanović's poetic, prosaic, and dramatic approach represents, in a unique sense, an array of basic concepts and elements of human existence, its earthly and cosmic destiny. He tackles the subjects of freedom, the Absolute, God, the Devil, chaos, order, truth, the world, etc. The philosophical, the religious, and the poetic make up the basic core in the interpretation and understanding of the ontology of human survival."

— *Jovo Cvjetković*

Contents

NOWHERENESS IN THE WORLD

THE COURT IN THE VOID

'Tis sad to be a king without a kingdom,
And even sadder – a kingdom without a king.

THE SMALL SKY AND THE BIG SKY

Inside the small sky
There is a big one

The small sky conceals it
Deep within

It keeps it safe from the void
Outside the world

So that the void won't engulf it
Once it inhabits the small sky

Once the small sky is bored with loneliness
It decides to receive the void

And rid itself of the burden
Of the big sky longing

For the road
And a journey into the void

Thus, the big sky is born
And sets out on a long journey

At the end of the road
The big sky converts into the small one

And the small sky
Locks it inside itself again

BLACK LIGHT

Darkness is an eternity asleep
Frozen beyond existence,
And light – a song in the fiery sweep –
Awakening, dawn, and existence.
Darkness is a winter that hides the light,
And light – a spring –
Darkness' salvation and hope;
Darkness is a powerful guardian of light,
While light guards darkness from darkness.
In the light, the eternity of the eternal
    Flower blossoms,
Looking forward to the journey and motion,
Looking forward to the court sprung from the void.
In the middle of the center, in the middle of the end
    Both inside and outside
There is an infinite temple of light
In the temple of darkness,
Infinite is the power of the ray
That keeps the eternal darkness at bay,
Endless are the paths,
Endless are the tales,
Endless are the bright beams,
Rays smiling from the heavens
In the middle of the night of oblivion,
In the middle of all shipwrecks,
From the terrible confusion of the world,
From the terrifying torment of being,
Accompanied by the howls of all the gods
Against the images of non-being
The light of the world is born
Flying both inward and out,

Permeating throughout
That ancient tower of being
Rising proudly
From non-being.
Even in flight, it still dreams,
About trails and seas,
About tales and gardens of paradise,
About its newborn youth,
About the infinite path
Sunlit by its rays;
It reminisces about its Father –
It always remembers its spark –
It remembers the dark ray
In which from the dusk, it hid away,
It remembers the comfort,
Eternities asleep,
It remembers the serenity,
The impeccable harmony
But it felt too constrained
To hide in the darkness
And stifle the all-seeing eyes
With desolate darkness from the desolate land;
That is why it lit up
In the middle of the night and emptiness;
That is why it embarked
On the bright path to its Court,
Its heavenly temple
That rises from the wasteland
To defy nothingness.

THE HEART OF THE WORLD

NOTHING HAS EVER HAPPENED

Nobody has gone anywhere
Nothing has ever happened
Only the dream has waited for us
To settle into it

Nobody is bigger than anyone else
Not a word to anyone will be said
About the little dream with no beginning
About the little heart that gave birth to everything

About the little Sun preceding all the suns,
The black source of light
About the lip kissing the emptiness
And waiting (eagerly) to impregnate it

About the anguish, pain, and beauty of desire
So that desire would light up,
The dream would turn into light
And dreaming in light would ensue

That everything is remembered by everything
And not a thing is overlooked
That everything forgets everything
And everything is erased

Nobody has gone anywhere
Nothing has ever happened
Only the dream has waited for us
To settle into it

THE OLD SOURCE

THE FIRST DREAM
A FAIRY

I often returned to the celestial homeland's starry landscape, within my foggy desires, recognizing the unknown contours and pondering the ultimate truth of things. Forests, fogs, and whirlpools rose above this thought, this enchantment, and this authentic place.

Along with this dream, another was born. In that dream, there was a woman nobody fully understood or described. The dream was about a fairy, Laura, Beatrice, the non-existent Helen, a cat woman, and a snake woman – a dream about all women and madnesses, jealousies, fears, passions, torments, and crimes committed because of women.

This secret of secrets and truth of truths hovers over us and in us, almost from times immemorial: the picture of the ideal, imagined woman not dreamed of enough, unattainable and unreachable. This picture replaces and enhances reality as if by God's creation: woman as an illusion, an obsession, a fulfillment of one's ego, an initiator, a paradox, and a destroyer.

On a hill where I often hiked, I sat down to rest and contemplate but fell asleep after a long walk and meditation. I caught sight of her contours in the mist. This enigmatic and somewhat melancholy beauty was approaching, moving closer and closer. She wore only a fog cloak, further emphasizing her dreamy curves. She touched me with her fingers. Trembling, I thought that my heart might jump from my chest. I woke up in a cold sweat but soon afterward fell asleep again.

The fog lifted, and I could see the town's shape below. There were attractive but strange streets as if haunted. Even to myself, I appeared as a stranger in the city, which should have been mine, but it seemed not to be. I then went to a park by the lake. The park was full of different flowers, and the lake was well known for its variety of birds.

Walking through the park, at one point, I decided to make a bouquet of the most beautiful flowers, which were growing everywhere. I reached the lake with a bouquet and started throwing small flat stones at the water, watching how they skipped along the water's surface, recalling how this was my favorite game in childhood. The small pebbles skimmed the farthest, almost reaching the island. One reached the island itself and ended up in the hand of the woman in the mist.

Shocked, I thought that this terrible dream belonged to the past, that I had woken up and liberated myself from this nightmare, but here again, she appeared. She was the most beautiful and captivating yet disturbing Being. Why is she here, in my city, and where did she acquire the skill to catch small stones with her tender hand effortlessly? Although it was evening and she was not that near, I saw her smile, and she invited me to join her.

I took a nearby rowboat and paddled to the island. I found myself on a deserted island, clearly recognizing that the woman was wearing only bright light, not mist. She flew above me, and I realized that she was a fairy. I have always wanted to meet a fairy.

FAIRY: People rarely come here.

– I often take walks through that park on the coast – pleasant nature, silence, meditation.

FAIRY: You like to dream?

– Passionately so. Is that good?

FAIRY: I think you like poetry, so I'll answer your question with a poem:

16

OUR DREAMS

As our thoughts begin the dream to unseal
While finding their way on the path of light,
Into the new thoughts, the day will conceal
The map showing every road to delight.
Dreams inside and around us, everywhere,
Thoughts dive in and instruct us – over there
Is where you should head to find the right way.
The dream keeps the thought from going astray
As dreams sometimes are left so desolate
By some who, in thoughts, slowly drift away.
Our dreams travel far and never abate.

As our thoughts paint with an earnest zeal
The fabulous day, meanwhile, in the night
A loyal dream does solemnly reveal
Grace, while shining over the path so bright.
In a livid dark, with delusions to spare,
The beacon of thoughts helps us with our fare.
And the thought that has burst out in a spray
Whispers to the dream to keep it at bay,
And everyone arrives someplace of late;
Every desire awash by the day –
Our dreams travel far and never abate.

As days announce a world ethereal,
We dream, out of obedience and fright,
That our dream won't be hopelessly unreal.
The day notes success in lucid insight,
In broad daylight, both our dream and hope glare
Growling like a cloud high up in the air:
Reality keeps dreams under its sway,

As thought hovers, slowly melting away.
In dreams, everyone's alike at any rate;
The light has dreams as its overlay.
Our dreams travel far and never abate.

The light of dreams is strewn in disarray,
The light sprinkled with our thoughts on display;
At the road's end, everyone finds their fate
For justice is studded with dreams at play.
Our dreams travel far and never abate.

- That means that our day and our path depend on our dreams.

FAIRY: What we dream becomes reality. But even if we achieve what we dream of, everything loses value if we do not feel it deep inside. Time plays an enormous role in this; time is not chased after but waited for during the breaks we take, as opposed to the races in which we lose what we chase. Only what you bring into yourself is yours.

- You don't believe in ownership?

FAIRY: The world cannot be owned. That is a delusion. Gods and animals do not know what private property is. Only people think they own things. The trick with which they achieve this is in their learning. People have educated themselves, built institutions, cadastral services, and banks, and through papers and signatures, managed to declare themselves the owners of what they claimed the right to, and they have managed to register it and make it official. The only thing that makes them the owners is their words and papers. In the same manner, they also think they own the land. But who can own land? That is absurd. People do not have a permanent claim on themselves, let alone the land. The land that is so much more powerful than humans; the land from which they were born, which created them, and to which they return. So how can they possibly be its owners when, if ownership exists at all, they are in its possession? People's deeds serve merely as a confirmation to other people and for other people and have nothing to do with actual ownership, which does not exist.

- What do you see as the solution?

FAIRY: Some ownership of time.

- How is that achieved? Please tell me a poem about it.

FAIRY:

A DAY OF THE YEAR

Fully at random, pick a day of the year
And dedicate it to yourself completely
Forget about the rush and all obligations
And reexamine yourself in solitude

On a green slope, where all is crystal clear,
In the true light, perhaps yourself, you will see
And renew your old sense of dedication
Perhaps in that peace, you'll find your fortitude

You'll see that you're alone and only one here
And in full charge of all your felicity,
All hopes, victories, and capitulations,
All your journey depends on your aptitude

In those green heights, all of your dreams will appear

To you from times of youthful simplicity
Keen to reap the fruit of new cultivation
That way, you'll find a new art with certitude

And you will surely see, somewhere very near,
Your dreams in full blossom of their sanctity,
Through the frozen moment, in navigation,
Aiding you to find light in plenitude

The whiteness of light you understand and hear
Springing from the very core of clemency
Whispering truth and novel revelations
About you finding your truth all renewed

To your verdant reveries, truth will adhere
Revealing in its flawless transparency
Brand new horizons, open destinations,
And that you'll map your road with exactitude

Before your eyes, in all its rosy veneer,
Your dream sprouts from the heart of leniency
You see your dreams in full realization
Soaring to reach unthinkable altitudes

All will be made known, everything will be clear,
Nature alone that is full of loyalty
Shares them with you in worldwide exploration –
Those from the past and those future will include

And the magic world before you reappears
To help you reemerge from your dormancy
Into a world – the best of all creation
That only in dreams can fully be pursued

And you pick flowers of this day's elation
Of a magnificent world in solitude

- That seems easy. Everybody thinks they can do it.

FAIRY: Everybody thinks they can do it, but they don't live that way. Everybody knows they have to take time to set aside a day occasionally, but even when they make that time, it is still not theirs. Nobody can defeat time. The only victory over time is the realization that it is undefeatable.

- You're right. But everyone thinks they know that, too.

FAIRY: What people think and verbally define does not necessarily have to comply with reality.

- Let's return to your tone and choice of words and adjectives. Why do you use words that may appear odd to the modern spirit, such as dreams, truth...? Everything seems too idealistic and easy. And life is neither one nor the other.

FAIRY: I am not talking about life itself, the games of life, or the movement through life. I am not talking about a day when the truth, which should guide one through life or offer all the solutions, will be displayed on the green carpet. I am talking about the day which is the sum of moments, self-awareness, and understanding of time in a way opposite to how people usually understand time.

People usually experience time as something they shall chase after. Regardless of the individual realization or material welfare, nobody can stop or capture time because it does not exist. Every race with it is futile and useless. What exists is life, not the abstract idea of time. In a deeper sense, no one can capture Life (or the movement of life) because it is inevitably transient. However, a moment of life can convey an epiphany that transcends the pleasure of current accomplishments, measured by comparison. If this criterion disappears, personal (dis)satisfaction and a sense of such accomplishment would also disappear. Still, greater satisfaction would arrive, measured by a larger, universal value system due to serendipitous moments acquired in this way.

I am talking about a single moment or a single day that does not open new paths (although that possibility remains), does not serve as a solution to the enigma, but rather enables concentration, regaining composure, meditation, immersion in a world of deeper essences, and merging with the flow of the universal moment and the spirit of the world. In this way, one does not chase after time but makes contact with life as a timeless entity, where the past and the future become part of the same – present – moment. In such a state, the individual gains ownership of himself as a source of the greatest possible wealth, which arises from the sense of unity with the world to which nothing he can add or from which nothing he can deduct. Everything that torments a person in everyday life disappears. That opens the door to spiritual peace, realization, and satisfaction.

The greatest misconception is the present moment because it becomes the past before we think of it. The present is virtually non-existent. A life that is at least to a certain extent unaware of the world and life as a timeless flow, in which the past and the future are not too delineated, loses even its present moment, which does not exist. Life is in constant transition between the past and the future. A day like this does not serve as a strategy for conquering the future and achieving practical goals, even though it indirectly and all but inevitably leads in that direction, but guides one toward merging in the timeless flow of the past and the future that's ever elusive, and which is the one true life.

If all these nouns, adjectives, or words seem too easy or obsolete, or their role seems didactic and practical, that is not the case. As a Fairy who lives beyond time and space, I speak what I truly think about it and what I find important. Only values are important. Everything valuable is time-free or timeless. Only through the establishment of values and a sense of value can the victory of life be a victory over time.

Only life passes, while time always remains the same. An accomplished life is a victory over time. Pursuing a goal and one's role in life is the most that can be expected and demanded of life. The sense of mere power or capital cannot compensate for the sense of harmony and magnificence of the world. This can satisfy vanity and provide comfort, but it cannot be a source of true happiness that comes from within – through the sense of harmony of the world and its wealth that transcends all earthly or individual wealth.

A day like this enables coping with life's past and future. A day like this outplays time, for it pursues life, not time. People have life, not time; what passes is not time but life. Humans have invented the concept of time to measure the passage of the world or life. Time only means motion. There is no time without motion. Time is not a special category, able to survive on its own. Without space, there is no time. There is neither space nor time in a worldless God or before the world's birth. Space and time create the possibility of a world in multitude. Multitude establishes relationships. Relationships provide space.

- But, Fairy, the tone of your poem and how you describe things using slightly saccharine adjectives leave the impression of a fairy tale. There is no such tone today. There is an everyday way of expression, studded with certain strange metaphors, to avoid the old ways of expression.

FAIRY: That is true. But, which is the old way of expression? Language is evolving and changing, yet the same ideas still live in people's minds. It is impossible to change completely the expression of something that remains the same throughout the ages. Art deals with the world and life, so art cannot maintain and seek its freshness and originality exclusively through the form and modification of language or its usage. Value is not achieved by mere experiment nor solely by a modern tone if its purpose is merely to be modern. In that sense, Homer, and especially Dante, as well as Shakespeare, are still modern in form, tone, and content from the perspective of any age. The great delusion and misconception of the twentieth-century artists was in the opinion that experiments in art had no bounds. In that case, art ceases to be real art, based on universal standards unchanged over time, and becomes a search for a concept. In that way, the concept becomes the goal of art, not its means, which is wrong.

Undoubtedly, Kazimir Malevich was an extraordinarily talented artist (this is merely one of the numerous examples), but his point on the canvas marked (along with many other phenomena) the announcement of the point on the path, or the canvas, of fine art. Many twentieth-century artists, especially visual artists, seemed to want to overlook time. And if time is overlooked to achieve a personal victory, the future is wasted without a good reason, and the future pays the price. Such a condition confuses and contributes to a latent, delayed chaos or downfall. However, all is not lost if there is a favorable climate and someone (an artist) puts up an unconditional fight, first and foremost for the victory of his profession and only afterward for a personal triumph. The artist's victory does not always coincide with the victory of art. That is how one reaches the point (the end) ahead of time. Undoubtedly, Picasso, Dali, de Chirico, Magritte, to name but a few artists, created works valuable from the historical perspective, but where can one go next? I don't claim, not yet at least, that this has happened or has to happen, but the situation is far from ideal when it comes to fine arts.

As for the written word, the situation is much better, but there has been a general decline in standards caused, among other things, by a futile struggle to achieve a modern expression at all costs – instead of striving for the realization of modern values – and the overall commercialization of all spheres of life, which affected art as well. Under such circumstances, many more mediocre artists appear, which also implies fewer quality works of art.

The key question is – how can the value be maintained or, if possible, improved, and not how can it be modern at all costs. Modernism, understood in this way, creates a false impression, or an illusion, of novelty, while in reality, the products of such an approach are most commonly not new at all. Even if they look modern and are mutually different, they all share the same impulse, which makes them unrecognizable despite their diversity on the surface. Those are works of art that, despite being seemingly different, are still made in the same mold, the only difference being dimension and decoration.

Doing this is much easier than striving for values by taking chances and undertaking the old challenges, which are approached in a new way in terms of content and ideas, not only formally. The fact that such an approach may seem less original is only an illusion caused by the insistence on the patterns we discussed earlier. Those patterns are generally accepted and valid, regardless of the grounding in the value, which, nevertheless, in everything and at all times must be the basic criterion. Real modernity implies value. What has no value cannot be modern just because it has a modern form, which is its own purpose.

Any undertaking that strives to win points in that way is insincere and cannot survive in time because, throughout history, only what was considered extremely valuable has managed to last. Without exception, what was extremely valuable was simultaneously modern or new. Not only do value and modernity not cancel each other out, but one cannot exist without the other. I don't mean to say that everything modern automatically becomes valuable. On the contrary, only what is valuable can be modern. Value is a condition of modernity. Modernity can only be a consequence of value and never, by no means, its self-sufficient condition.

Modernity is born as a natural consequence of a certain period, even when we speak of the program and stylistic orientation, not as a consequence of overly individual concepts without a universal value. Self-serving modernism is no modernism but a struggle for a personal victory. Modernism that serves value is the only true modernism, for it fights not for the triumph of personal value but for one that is universal, articulated through a personal expression that represents it in the best possible way. Everything valuable also contains some novelty, a precondition for a work of art that becomes modern as an expression of the new value.

Therein lies the difference between the fashionable and the modern. A modern expression, or form, serves content and, as such (if successful), becomes a value in itself. On the other hand, the fashionable, which is often mistakenly identified with the modern despite the repudiations from its protagonists, is an expression of a false novelty flirting with the spirit of the times. That kind of false modernism does not strive for high art. Still, the victory of expression or a concept, although appearing original at first glance, is not sublime because it arises from the matrix of misunderstood or misused ideas of modernism. That suits many because it is easier and opens the door to mediocrity. However, the result is a relativization of values and profiting from gimmicks or jokes that serve to provide theoretical confirmation and argumentation by theorists who thus open the door to mediocrity. That creates a vicious circle, the victims of which are high art and potential top artists.

- Such a situation opens the door to chaos.

FAIRY: Yes. Because unfettered freedom is no freedom at all. Art should be a consequence of organic development, not of patterns imposed from outside, which are then enforced and justified by individual concepts. Any change in art must be justified by value. Otherwise, what is born will not be able to justify itself by vain modernity or unfounded concepts.

Freedom is achieved through discipline, and discipline implies rules, effort, understanding, and a display of talent through value that is not accidental. The concept must be an expression of something deeply rooted. Excessive freedom leads to losing freedom, not to its realization or inauguration. Behind every success, there must be effort, which implies limited freedom. Every personal success is based on self-restriction of personal freedoms. That kind of restriction yields results that are the only source of freedom. The world of total freedom is neither a world of freedom nor justice; it is a world of chaos and decay. From the standpoint of the individual, it is a world of personal decay and unfulfillment, where the surplus of freedom, which is understood in that way, leaves the individual devoid of freedom. Unfulfillment is not a source of freedom but a source of slavery. Fulfillment, only possible through self-restraint, leads to the highest degree of freedom.

In the chaos, order is achieved through law. Everything in nature operates according to law. Those laws establish the functioning of the natural organism and maintain a hierarchy of values in nature. Decrees and documents do not establish that, but the functioning of the natural organism contains the law, or laws, on every level. Nothing in nature can voluntarily decide to change those laws or abolish them. Those laws are a kind of cosmic order established through the disciplined working of natural laws. Any disturbance within this system leads not to freedom but decay, collapse, and entropy.

The road to freedom, within the framework of the natural system, including both society and the individual, leads through the establishment of order and a system that works and can only work in an order in which everything has a proper place. The planets can't say, "We want freedom" and escape from the stars. This is not a matter of choice because if so, everything in nature would likely disperse even before establishing the order of nature or the world. Laws in nature cannot be opposed, and they regulate everything. There is some dictatorship of natural laws without which there would not be order out of chaos or within chaos, without which freedom would not be possible because opposition to those laws does not imply freedom but decay.

- People believe they have clarified, to a great degree, the question of the relationship between discipline and freedom. I, too, was convinced to have a pretty original opinion on this (despite it being logical and requiring only common sense) until I found out that many educators today, and even doctors and some cardinals, like Cardinal Ruini (a former vicar of the Roman Diocese), spread those ideas.

FAIRY: All of them, consciously or unconsciously, rely rather heavily on John Dewey *(Democracy and Education),* who explained those ideas, even though, unfortunately, he is still insufficiently understood or even misunderstood.

- Jeremy Bentham created a draft and gave a theoretical and philosophical *(Panopticon)* basis for what troubled Foucault and what he tried to unmask in *Discipline and Punish.* Perhaps the key is in the understanding of the term – interest. The title of the tenth chapter of Dewey's book is – "Interest and Discipline."

FAIRY: Individuals can exercise their interests best only through discipline. On the other hand, society (which shouldn't necessarily be equated with the state or government) cannot exercise its interests best without discipline. The formula lies in reconciling the interests of the individual with those of society, but not to the detriment of one or another. The greater the harmony between the individual interests and those of society, the greater the harmony is within society, while the individual's position improves exponentially. In this relation, the only thing possible is the functioning of democracy as a still insufficiently realized ideal. The harmony between the interests of the individual and those of society depends on the degree of democracy or the realization of ideals.

If self-interest is the primary motivation, regardless of personal value, society suffers, and vice versa. It is the same in the field of art. Art suffers if an artist insists on personal artistic interest, concept, or taste, regardless of value. The degree of value of a particular work depends on the compliance of an artist's interests with the superior demands of art. Such achievements are only possible through personal discipline, which imposes the criterion.

Considering that phenomena in art and science differ from those in society, what can be democratic in a society becomes distinctly undemocratic in art because it leads to a degradation of standards.

People achieve significant results in many professions through hard work and mechanical use of the craft. In art and science, work is associated with the talent and unique characteristics of the artist and the scientist, which set them apart from other people and enable different results, regardless of the invested effort, in proportion to the power of the artist or the scientist.

All artists and scientists, or authors of any kind, who feel in such a way, consciously or unconsciously, desire, conditionally speaking, "the democratization of art." In that way, the range between the unwritten canon of high art or value and personal artistic interests or strengths becomes blurred without any guarantee of exceptional value or art that will come out from such views and approaches. Thus, the effect becomes opposite to what can often be desirable and democratic in society. That effect is manifested in the rule of personal interests, which reduces the possibility of attaining superior value. Such an atmosphere gives birth to a larger number of artists and authors but a smaller number of quality works of art. The result of such tendencies would mark the victory of the mediocre, who could exclaim: "I have won and earned my right, my value, and my understanding." The only problem is that even if, in that case, the individual is victorious, or a number of them are, art loses nevertheless. In the field of art, democracy implies the death of supreme value. The consequences are disastrous because they inevitably lead to the decline of cultural standards and, as a consequence, of the standards of democracy in society; there is a decline in the possibility of striving for an ideal or realizing the social ideal. Total democracy is the death of democracy.

- But the world is constantly changing; understanding of the world and art and its function all change.

FAIRY: Perhaps there is a reason why people cannot see the true state of affairs at a given moment. They cannot step out of their frame to observe the moment and realize that sometimes there is a crisis of creativity, and sometimes it is just impossible to continue in the old fashion, while the new one does not promise high achievements. In music, for example, everybody loves the Beatles, and many consider or would like them to be on par with Mozart and Beethoven. Still, everyone feels that it is impossible and ridiculous. Everything has its course, including society and art. Standards cannot be maintained by mechanical transplantation of the old models or artificial creation of the new ones.

Throughout history, high art has been, above all, the supreme reflection of its time, expressed in the language and concepts of its time. If Shakespeare had wanted to be Homer, he would have become neither Homer nor Shakespeare. That is not merely a matter of talent, knowledge, and skills but of common sense. Shakespeare could not think like Homer, although he had a similar range, because Homer was predisposed, by his time, to understand and experience the world differently – not only formally but also conceptually and linguistically. Homer's experience of the world, and the experience of the people from the ancient times for whom his message was, is different from the modern one; it is even significantly different from the experiences and concepts of the world soon to come. Some ancient Greek lyrical poets like Sappho, Archilochus, and Anacreon, who lived merely two or three centuries after Homer, have more in common with your time in a conceptual sense (in terms of the body-soul relationship, for example) than with Homer.

Language is changing, as is the function of language, the concepts expressed by language, and the very function of art and its use. The function of Homer's songs was not the same or, at the very least, was not realized, nor could it be as it is today. Today, the written word is more important than the spoken one, and in that sense, the art of the written word can be different and expressed in another way, yet it would achieve the same purpose for modern people as the old way achieved for the ancient people.

- It is strange how things change over time without us being aware of it most of the time. For example, the eighteenth century in Spanish poetry did not exist virtually. And yet it did, with the same number of poets as in other periods, and probably many of them were convinced that they were not inferior to the poets of earlier times; however, any respectable anthology of Spanish poetry overlooks the eighteenth century.

FAIRY: There was not a single Spanish poet in the eighteenth century to rise above the existing mannerisms, although Spanish poetry, in general, did reach peaks comparable to those of other major European cultures and produced some extraordinary talent in the twentieth century, including poets from other Spanish-speaking countries.

- The biggest problem seems to arise when people, or artists, fight too hard for personal victory, as you claim. By doing so, they end up stifling the opportunities for the highest achievements in every period and field of creative human endeavor. That is the case when

31

personal interest is above merit or interest of any particular field of human endeavor.

FAIRY: Although paradoxical, knowledge, or the illusion of one, is the main contributor to dogmatism and manipulation, especially in modern societies that have achieved some mass literacy and mass acquisition of knowledge. Such knowledge has enabled the formation of mini-totalitarianisms. Everybody is focused on the totalitarian nature of Nazism, Communism, and any other kind of fundamentalism. Yet, everybody forgets that mini-totalitarianisms operate in societies, hidden behind unions, human rights advocacy, fight for democracy, freedom, political appropriateness or correctness, religious blocks, and similar. What creates the illusion that those mini-totalitarianisms are not dangerous lies in the fact that none of them is universal totalitarianism under the auspices of the state (even though many are so). That does not make them any less dangerous; quite on the contrary. It is so because they are better camouflaged and thus potentially more efficient and dangerous.

- Such a situation contributes to the deterioration of standards.

FAIRY: Indeed. Because all the representatives of mini-totalitarianisms fight exclusively, or mostly, for their idea. The matter is further complicated by their conviction that they are right, while often they only believe they are. Their common starting point, however, is the interest of each block, regardless of to what extent the philosophical discourse by which those tendencies are defended can be knowledge-based, nuanced, and convincing.

- Harold Bloom was right to emphasize the aesthetic criterion when evaluating literature. In *The Western Canon,* he strives to preserve value by highlighting the top achievements of literature, regardless of how hopeless the whole struggle is, considering the modern tendencies that generally lead to the breaking of the canon. With the same goal in mind, some thirty years ago, at a round table where revolutionary poetry was discussed, I claimed that a poem could only be revolutionary according to the aesthetic, not the thematic criteria. The topic is subservient to aesthetics, not vice versa.

FAIRY: Those tendencies, or mini-totalitarianisms, lead to glorifying all that goes in favor of the agenda of any of those tendencies, even in art. On the other hand, there are market requirements, which are also unregulated and guided by aesthetic criteria. Consequently, little room is left to nurture the art of superior quality.

- Mass culture, mass influences, and new media play a big part in this.

FAIRY: Society is inevitably changing, and consequently, so are art, beliefs, and the application of art. Not even in the past did everything work out in favor of high art, but there were no mass influences of another kind, and thus, art was more or less unhindered to fulfill its role. In modern societies, a person is under a constant barrage of various influences, which people find difficult to defend themselves from despite their best efforts. Modern times have produced a kind of omniscient ignoramus or a cultured savage. He acquires knowledge, but not culture, not in the true sense; he knows "a lot" yet understands little; he judges without developed criteria; his criteria are based on the relativization of the value embedded in him by modern education systems and the mass media. He thinks within the pop culture constraints and looks at the world and art from inside this frame, unable to change the perspective.

- Art has always changed. What we remember and understand as the historical pinnacles of music have lasted merely a few centuries and ended at the beginning of the twentieth century. Other arts, or expressions within the framework of particular arts, have changed drastically. Matthew Arnold made an interesting observation about poetry and the novel based on the etymology of the words *verse* and *novel*, which come from the words *versus* and *novus*. *Versus* (the verb *vertere*) designates something opposite, repetitive, recursive, while *novus* means novelty (eng. *novel,* from Italian *novella,* from the same word – *novella* from Vulgar Latin, from *novelus, novus*). Poetry lives in the repetition of the refrain or rhymes (to put it quite simply), while the novel most commonly deals with novelties in the broadest sense of the word. That indicates the organic development of the form, which is by no means accidental.

FAIRY: Prose also flourished in ancient times (in a way, novels did as well), but novels first appeared, in the modern sense of the word, with Cervantes. *Prose (prosus)* and *versus* are Latin words. However, prose has always been considered a more ordinary, less concise, and generally easier to grasp, more accessible mode of expression.

Following the historical development of literary forms, we conclude that without Seneca, we would probably have never had Montaigne's essays, which opened the door to this particular literary genre. Also, without Seneca, there would have been no Elizabethan drama (including Marlowe and Shakespeare) as we know it, even though the best Elizabethan authors were incomparably better playwrights than Seneca.

- But the situation with music is different. There was no Mozart or Beethoven in antiquity, nor was there anyone to rival them in the time of Saint Augustine or Thomas Aquinas. And would Bach and the composers who succeeded him have been possible without polyphony (which appeared in the late Middle Ages and at the beginning of the Renaissance) and counterpoint (from the late Renaissance and Baroque)?

FAIRY: Even without those inventions, there would certainly have been great musical achievements, but the world of music would have been incomparably less complete and underdeveloped. However, the concept of polyphony had existed even earlier. Although music at the time of the ancient Greeks was monophonic, we can conclude, based on Plato's observations, that at the time, new musical ideas appeared, to which Plato objected, believing that they arose out of a desire for reputation and popularity. In his opinion, such tendencies led to a violation of the musical law and the establishment of theatrocracy instead of music aristocracy. However, Aristoxen was among the first to oppose the strict formal requirements and Pythagoras' ideas about musical harmony.

Counterpoint is, in fact, a term that originated in the fourteenth century, while polyphony, in the form of diphony, appeared in the ninth century or even earlier. Composers Léonin (twelfth century) and Pérotin (thirteenth century) belonged to the Notre Dame School of Polyphony. The answer to whether great composers, from Monteverdi through Bach, Beethoven, and Mozart, would have been able to express fully the strength of their genius without those inventions is – no.

However, the background of this question is not simple because it leads to another question: Would those musical geniuses be able to invent those technical elements? Theoretically – yes; in practice – probably not. Those ingenious artists possessed an abundance of pure artistic and musical genius, which enabled them to express, in the best way, their power within those already established music systems, and they could make the most of the latest inventions. All that arose as a consequence of the development and contribution of a large number of people over a long period. The restoration of the classical ideal did not affect only fine arts but also music since the concepts of the ancient Greeks were perceived as a novelty. Something that had existed two thousand years earlier – became a novelty. That fact says a lot about society and how easily society can stagnate or even regress.

However, it is theoretically possible to imagine a person who can be credited with the invention of polyphony or counterpoint. It is also possible to imagine them producing trifle musical works. Despite that, theoretically speaking, without him (or her), many subsequent superior works based on those achievements would not have been possible, nor would great composers have been able to express and prove their genius by composing them. Who is a true genius, then? In the example created for this purpose, the author of that which enables the emergence and better expression of ingenious power creates only minor works. Still, without him or her, none of those geniuses would have existed.

"What is important in art?" doesn't seem to be the simplest of questions. This particular (imagined) or collective musical genius created what none of the most eminent composers managed to create (or probably even could). Without those achievements, the individual genius of the great composers would not have been able to achieve full flair, expression, and articulation. Each of the great composers, especially from the Baroque to the present day, employed the technique invented by an unknown genius, without which neither of them would have been accomplished. That means that without this individual or collective genius, the emergence of many geniuses would not be possible, while he obviously could emerge without them. He depends on them much less than they do on him. This is the question of the authorship of invisible value that is omnipresent yet constantly overlooked.

It would take twenty centuries after Homer for Dante to appear (with Virgil standing midway). Who was the one to come up with the idea of a hexameter and the way of thinking, not merely poetry writing, without which it would have been impossible to have Homer and all those for whom he was a role model? It's easy to imagine that this phenomenon, which was instrumental in the emergence of Homer, was the deed of the collective and individual genius of anonymous masters. Without Homer, there would not have been only other great ancient Greek poets but also hexameters in Latin, and, finally, there would be no Virgil either. So on, the tale of development continues to unfold.

- Parmenides and Empedocles expressed their philosophical ideas in verse.

FAIRY: They did. The functional difference between verse and prose was not as conspicuous as today. That is why Lucretius could easily communicate the ideas of stoicism in verse while creating a work of exceptional poetic value.

- Homer sang his verses accompanied by a lyre, which was music in the service of atmosphere. One can wonder whether anyone who listened to Homer enjoyed it more than Cioran did while listening to Beethoven (in connection with his remark that life would be meaningless without top musical achievements). The very sensual and cognitive experience changes.

FAIRY: Cioran probably read Nietzsche too early, who claimed that "without music, life would be a mistake." Cioran was irreparably sad regardless of the books he read or his wit (just as, on the other hand, Democritus always smiled and, after an examination, Hippocrates determined that he was not insane but liked to laugh by predisposition); however, it is a fact that other people's ideas can be disastrous if they are accepted and understood superficially. The problem is often not in ideas but in their misunderstanding.

A new time, based on the historical course, can win the right to new artistic forms. Still, art may disappear, although it's hard to imagine it. However, it is pretty easy, and even desirable, to imagine the birth of new artistic forms or a synthesis of the old ones; the birth of the new, not exclusively through experiment regardless of the value, which was a great delusion of the twentieth century, but of the new that is a natural product of the time in which one lives. Of the new, through research and realization not only within the framework of form or expression but also of the creation of new literary and artistic forms as an organic consequence of time.

If historical development has led toward change, then change is necessary because humans, as art consumers, also change. Not only is everything named but what is named is named so well in supreme works of art throughout history that it makes no sense to repeat things. On the other hand, creating art from too personal a vision, in which spoons, forks, and plates would be the ultimate artistic items, also makes no sense.

A way forward can also be a way back. You have passed through the phase of idolatry of science, but the difference between artistic, scientific, philosophical, and religious thoughts may diminish. Art and science could go back to their original roots in terms of the understanding that their root is the same and unique.

You don't know enough about the Mycenaean culture, and could Homer possibly exist without it? There was no drama or lyrical poetry in Homer's time. To a large extent, he served as the basis for developing lyrical poetry, drama, and philosophy. All the elements of drama occur in Homer, including the catharsis. Grammar and thought processes were perfected by Homer's technical mastery and caesuras of his hexameter; his prosody greatly surpasses the technical dimension of mastery. If we look for an example of nobility and sublimity, in addition to artistic value, we cannot find a better example than Homer.

- It seems certain and clear that the poetic word enabled the development of religion and philosophy (from which sciences will arise).

FAIRY: But it is unclear if humans obtained a new instrument and a kind of new sense, a super-sense through words. Without words, and in addition to the invention of the wheel or a way to start a fire, humans would remain at the level of other animals (if they survived at all) or, in the best case, at the level of savages (even with the cave paintings). Above all, the word enabled the development of thoughts and ideas. Once they mastered the ideas, humans became the masters of the planet, and it was virtually impossible to go back afterward.

Humans can progress or regress through stages, but they can't go back unless they abuse (or forget) their thoughts and ideas to an extreme degree or become victims of natural catastrophes or wars.

The original form of the articulated expression of ideas had to be some prayer or incantation, a song. Even if the purpose was religious, the method was artistic. Religious consciousness or influence is impossible without words' magical effect. The magical effect of words can only be achieved through art. That is how poetry was created. And that was the basis for the development of religion and philosophy. (That is why the *Bible* is, first and foremost, a poetic text.)

That kind of speech articulation brought humans into contact with nature and the universe. In search of answers, humans sharpened their thoughts through magical or poetic use of language. That was the basis of philosophy. Afterward, the sciences emerged from it.

Perhaps in the future, we should decrease those differences to achieve cultural continuity and maintain genuine progress in a society that is not and cannot be merely technological but value-centered, revolving around essential questions of existence.

The materialistic civilization is based on relying exclusively, or to the greatest possible extent, on the technological course and is essentially anti-cultural. The danger would have been smaller if it was just anti-culture. On the contrary, there is a culture, but culture is not its goal; its exclusive goal is the vulgar power of money. It takes merely a few generations for such tendencies to turn people into cultural savages who possess knowledge yet experience nothing *(Brave New World)*. The result of such tendencies would be reflected in the loss of interest in the deeper existential content and values and, consequently, in the greatest literature and art. In these circumstances, the omniscient ignoramus would set up cultural criteria, while the cultured (literate) savage would be a new enthusiast and consumer of art.

- If I understand you correctly, one needs to take a break to observe the path on our journey. In that sense, I'd like you to tell me about that journey and your world beyond space and time.

FAIRY: Gladly:

THE PATH OF THE WORLD

The world glimmers, the path does quake
Living in the very same place
Movement is a mere illusion
There's no path into the void's domain

With the mortal coil shed with grace,
One returns to whence he once came
One can't tell the goal from the start
All paths lead to one conclusion

The beam calls darkness by the name
There is no going forth or back
The world is in feverish haste
To birth a sky that stands apart

Even face-to-face with pitch-black,

The world, a hunter and its prey,
Devours void while sinking within
In self-pursuit, relentlessly paced

When the path wipes the void away
The illusions are again no more,
Into itself, the world retreats
Weary of being worn so thin

When it wanders off way too far
It sinks in, sightless and opaque,
Until it settles on its plain
To hide again and stay discreet

- We must return to the old sources, to the all-uniting spring.

FAIRY: That is true.

THE OLD SOURCE

Rekindle the old source's flame
To find a path through each wilderness:
Your flame is your guide, and you are the pass.

In your mind, you are never out of the frame
There's always some opening in some recess
Rekindle the old source's flame.

What others give to me, as I want to do the same,
Is almost always a mere bit of randomness,
Which desire transforms into a way to express it.
Rekindle the old source's flame.

FAIRY: Now tell me about some of your experiences that look from beyond space and time.

- With pleasure:

THE THIRD EYE

Through the car windows, I can see skyscrapers rise;
A secret was unveiled just when I closed my eyes;
From Thessaloniki, I'm back to my homeland;
A new image in my mind just began to rise.

Thessaloniki suburbs are now far away
My head cannot seem to remember night or day,
Strange whirls of images are raging in my mind,
Turning it into a vast stage set for a play.

Places I've visited are trivial and dull;
Impact made by images nothing can annul;
I see the buildings of another world afloat –
All those cities are but a large yet empty hull;

I see strange letters all over the buildings' walls,
Perhaps Chinese or from another world, they all
Count my pictures as if wondering who reads them
In a world devoid of sight and hues of the fall.

THE EYE OF CONSCIOUSNESS

We like things of old –
Great ranges they hold;
All forgotten truths
Our thoughts will behold.

Pictures less than clear –
From dreams, there appear
Phantoms and past lives
With all they held dear;

We like things gone by,
Gone from the mind's eye;
Love them, for we know
What one can espy.

Deep inside the mind
Dreams a world refined;
All that comes from grace
Is of the best kind.

DEJAN STOJANOVIĆ

THE DAY IN THE MIDDLE OF THE PATH

Hopeful, I sprightly go into the day;
The open space between the world and me
Reveals a dream in glorious display.

There is no deception or memory;
Bemused by flight, enchanted, under sway,
Amid the path, the day intercepts me;

I am drunk, yet so awake in a way,
Change makes my blood boil with intensity,
The salty taste of the sea has worn away,

Lunar phases I observe with apathy
On the path, I chase the loyal sunray,
Drowsy eyes are almost all I can see;

Under a small, bright world's constant survey,
I am armed and rewarded handsomely
With a thousand looks, all those eyes betray

With Supreme Vision's unmatched clarity
I count and leave the foul world in dismay
Along with nights of sleepless agony.

SHELLS AND SNAILS

All shellfish possess such weird frames,
We listen to them all the same,
Looking for them within the frame
Of sandy shores;
Hide them in drawers that contain
What came before.

Snails with shells they carry around
Prance all over the sandy ground,
Dragging along the sky they found
Into the bright world,
And dance in the meadows unbound –
They twist and twirl.

All those little shellfish and snails
Are courts that only dreams unveil
Through which noises unbounded trail
In summer's prime.
They are paths down which small worlds sail
To the sublime.

- May I ask you now to sing to me something specific about the
values you speak of?

FAIRY: All right.

CORONA

CORONA

Transforming these words into purest light,
Invisible glow of darkness giving,
Weary day of its burden relieving,
With nothing but words, I make darkness bright;
Out of all words creating light's abode,
Speckles of light, by way of melody
Invading; with the sound of clemency,
Alchemy of creation I decode.

Only beauty has light and warmth to share;
While what is unknown is fated to die
Of oblivion, unable to repair
The world that fades before its time is nigh.
Words are the light and force, for sure;
Words are what I choose to help me endure.

THE HELP

Words are what I choose to help me endure –
They are a balm and a lucky charm's spark,
Words shine bright even when the day is dark.
In their meaning, there hides the power pure
Of the day that will surely never end,
World that, even in darkness, perseveres,
One through which the core of the secret sears,
One from which the eternal day extends.

Take another step; you surely can't be
Far from the secret of the Source from where
Once you emerged in luminosity;
Swim this vast ocean, where only a few dare;
The stronger your strokes – the longer the day;
Swim strongly toward your daydreaming way.

SWIM STRONGLY

Swim strongly toward your daydreaming way,
From your dream offer the world a ray of light;
In dreams, every single thing is woven tight –
The dream gives birth to both your and my day.
Everything is within reach of the thoughts
Unafraid of the darkness's abyss,
Of light that's concealed in the darkest bliss,
Or chromatic playtime all but forgot.

Dive into the water, head for the pearl
Of the unknown shell, find your way around,
Rejoice in the midst of the marine hurl,
Do not lose your head when troubles abound.
Disasters can sometimes act as road signs:
Trouble shows paths to those with open minds.

TROUBLE

Trouble shows paths to those with open mind.
The gales and raging seas are but a test;
Call yourself a seaman and give your best,
Trouble will show you the peace you need to find;
When your mind dives all the way to the floor
Of a sea deeper than reality
To stay away from cheap frivolity,
Measuring the world by a higher score.

And there will be no unsettled accounts
When the goal feeds you – the shore will await,
And just up until the final showdown,
A calm port is there when the gale abates.
You choose the path – a sailor hard to match;
Hunter does not have beasts but himself to catch.

THE HUNTER

Hunter has not beasts but himself to catch;
The forest is a test and a source of food;
There, the beasts are your guardians for good;
Beasts give you strength and a goal to attach.
What's quickly gained has no value at all;
Without the beasts, the world would soon end,
Dark would be way too hard to comprehend.
Hunter's advantage lies in strain and fall.

Without beasts, you'd lose your way in the sleep
Of the dead sea, with no will to move on
To the hidden spoils at the ocean's deep,
Goal you'll be likely forced to abandon.
Only a byroad leads to a treasure –
All that's hard-earned is genuine pleasure.

THE DANGER

All that's hard-earned is genuine pleasure;
Price of victory is effort, not joy;
Whatever in game and fight you employ
Is your greatest value and your treasure.
"What awaits you there just behind the bend?"
Is the question on Hunter's worried mind,
An unknown fighter of the sincere kind,
A sage looking down from a higher end.

There is no right path to be seen en route
By a light-farer in his finest hour,
Whom the very road directs in pursuit,
Whose gait is the source of sacred power.
Fear is the mortal danger to all life –
Splendor lies in brave partaking in strife.

COURAGE

Splendor lies in brave partaking in strife,
On many journeys, a reward will come,
A resolution of a conundrum,
Mind's nobility and grace that is rife.
Each path is a trap, a reward as well;
Joy is by way of learning well deserved,
Each danger defeated, and justice served
With the strength, that inside the heart does swell.

The sublime thought will guide you properly
On the path of light, to a higher grasp
Which bears new words before it sets them free
To shine when not even dormant Gods' gasp
Is heard. That's why with a modicum of might
I transform these words into purest light.

FAIRY: Now you should sing a song to me about something you
find important.

TERZA CORONAE

AWAKENING OF THE DAY
1

On a calm eve, without the moon in sight,
A sudden flash appeared inside my mind:
With pure force, it halved the terrible night,

Daydreaming of great glory, it will find
That secretly shines even in the dark;
A sudden flash appeared inside my mind –

Dark that awakes in me a sudden spark;
The whole world breaks open before my eyes –
One dark secretly shines in other dark.

My thoughts sail away through the night and rise
Nourished by light of the world from within –
The whole world breaks open before my eyes.

There's no day or dark, nowhere to begin;
Through the darkness, the luminous thought sears
Nourished by light of the world from within.

Darkness begins to falter, disappear –
On a calm eve, without the moon in sight,
Through the darkness, the luminous thought sears –
With pure force, it halved the terrible night.

2

A sudden flash appeared inside my mind,
Through the night, toward the light, I advanced
Watched by the night that was strongly inclined

Toward the day on which in dreams I chanced;
The night relented and was in retreat;
Through the night, toward the light, I advanced.

I saw my glow open every discreet
Nocturnal shelter, giving birth to day;
The night relented and was in retreat.

To the night around me, loyal I'll stay;
My mind's ablaze and eager to entreat
Nocturnal shelter, giving birth to day.

A nocturnal eye watches me discreet,
The extinguished sea is turning azure;
My mind's ablaze and eager to entreat

A nocturnal frame in a bright downpour.
A sudden flash appeared inside my mind –
The extinguished sea is turning azure;
Watched by the night that was strongly inclined.

3

The world secretly shines e'en in the dark –
All rays of the hidden nocturnal foam
Burst from the mind to give the world a spark.

A dark before a dark retreats alone,
The truth of the day penetrates the world –
All rays of its hidden nocturnal foam

Reveal the dark and touches undeterred;
Devoid of touch, the world's weak and forlorn –
The truth of the day penetrates the world.

I dissolve myself so the world is born,
I touch the darkness and the emptiness
Devoid of touch, the world's weak and forlorn.

This love inspires complete distress,
Darkness takes in the world that was in flight,
I touch the darkness and the emptiness.

Thus, the source of my day is the dark light,
To make the dark world shimmer in the dark;
Darkness takes in the world that was in flight,
Bursts from the mind to give the world a spark.

4

The whole world breaks open before my eyes:
The light of my mind comes back straight to me,
To sail the world under the mind's disguise;

To light the face of the dark entity –
Harmony's two primary hemispheres;
The light of my mind comes back straight to me.

In the night, the world, through rays, perseveres
In the sea of darkness, a light foam floats –
Harmony's two primary hemispheres.

Does light ever show in darkness's thoughts
When darkness is sad, lightless in the void?
In the sea of darkness, a light foam floats,

Spreading through the space valley unspoiled,
Conquering space in darkness to hover,
When it is sad and lightless in the void.

The light's thought culls a dark from another,
The whole world breaks open before my eyes,
Conquering space in darkness to hover,
To sail the world under the mind's disguise.

5

Nourished by light of the world from within,
The darkness finds shelter inside the light;
Thus, the day, number, and note all begin.

Calculation into the world alights,
The secret world diffuses all around,
The darkness finds shelter inside the light.

Darkness senses what days in dreams have found,
Light spreads around what the darkness once knew –
The secret world diffuses all around.

Because of the day it was to pursue,
Darkness broke cover, gave itself away –
Light spreads around what the darkness once knew.

Inside itself, the darkness hid the day
(The light of darkness is a sacred grace) –
It broke cover and gave itself away.

Darkness is the mother of flight and days,
Nourished by light of the world from within;
The light of darkness is a sacred grace;
Thus, the day, number, and note all begin.

6

The enlightened thoughts of the highest priest,
Fertilize the dark and give birth to days –
Truth burns words into the world to persist,

It sends out turbulent waves on their way
To spread the word of the truth all around,
Fertilize the dark and give birth to days.

The whole world turns into a touch unbound,
Into orgies of great ferocity,
To spread the word of the truth all around,

To offer life from white infinity,
To give birth, to fertilize and seduce
In an orgy of great ferocity.

A World into a World Thoughts introduce
To shine from the darkness and suns so bright
To give birth, to fertilize, and seduce.

The enlightened thoughts of the highest priest –
Truth burns words into the world to persist
To shine from the darkness and suns so bright
On a calm eve, with a full moon in sight.

A CONVERSATION BETWEEN DARKNESS AND LIGHT
1

Darkness and light have a conversation.
The bright thoughts dive into the emptiness;
The darkness gives them a warm reception.

Darkness:
You dive into my deep and dark expanse;
One without the other, we can't exist;
Your thoughts dive straight into the emptiness;

Darkness awakens your sanctuaries
To spread the day through my blank existence;
One without the other, we can't exist.

When you see yourself far in the distance,
You realize that I am your homeland;
You spread the day through my blank existence.

When you see me – you're saved, world without end;
Through your every thought, I diffuse outright;
You realize – I am your true homeland.

The darkness divests the day of its light;
Dies in darkless days since their inception;
The dark diffuses through her thoughts outright;
The darkness gives them a warm reception.

2

Your thoughts dive straight into the emptiness;
My only truth is what you are to me,
I begin to shine when the days regress.

I'm but light void of luminosity;
In me, there sleeps the origin of you;
My only truth is what you are to me;

When you light up, I turn completely blue;
My color entirely on you depends;
In me, there sleeps the origin of you;

The thought brings you into my hinterland;
On the path of light, I'm your watchful guard;
My color entirely on you depends;

I flow into you, mightily inward;
As emptiness into the day is born;
In my dark, dreams of your day I record;

I awake your light, dormant and forlorn.
Your thoughts dive straight into the emptiness
And emptiness into the day is born,
And I start to shine when the days regress.

3

We can't exist one without the other;
Without me, you would disappear within.
The day springs from the primary order.

You would stop looking for yourself therein
If there was no void from the day to shine;
Without me, you would disappear within.

In every ray, the dark lights up sublime
There is no world, day, or exultation
If there is no void from the day to shine.

With light's darkness, you hide retribution
Aimed at nothingness threatening your world.
There is no world, day, or exultation.

Everything here needs everything unfurled;
I am the empty house of your light ray
Of the nothingness threatening your world.

Beam flies into its home through the airway;
We can't exist one without the other;
I am the empty house of your light ray;
The day springs from the primary order.

4

To spread the day through my blank existence,
For the world to burst out in the dark's light
And dwell on the dark, limitless expanse.

Darkness hides within a world very bright;
Dark strays so that the world could stay on course,
So the world could burst out in the dark's light,

At the end of the dark path, it endorsed
In its own light, the dark begins to shine;
Dark strays so that the world could stay on course,

So light could absorb the darkness divine –
From its own light, the darkness radiates –
In its own light, the dark begins to shine.

Submerged in the world, dark joyfully bathes,
Glitters from within the world's edifice;
Dark flows into light streams and dissipates.

The world gushes out on the dark surface
To spread the day through my blank existence,
To gleam from within the world's edifice
And blaze on the dark, limitless expanse.

5

You realize that I am your homeland;
A tree sprouts from the bright darkness's soil –
And there appeared a glowing stretch of land.

A tree grows out of the dark's ray unspoiled;
Darkness watches over light in the light;
A tree sprouts from the bright darkness's soil –

Birth of the oldest Sun in all its might;
It could not radiate without darkness;
There's no day without darkness's birthright.

The joyful darkness speaks and undresses,
Sheds the dark clothes for the truth to unveil
Which cannot radiate without darkness.

The sun begins to shine in the world's dale;
Emptiness brimming with light that abounds
Sheds the dark clothes for the truth to unveil.

A bright rain falls and glimmers all around;
You realize that I am your homeland –
Emptiness brimming with light that abounds –
And there appeared a glowing stretch of land.

6

Through your every thought, I diffuse outright;
Without me, the mind is devoid of space
To scatter thoughts over seas of delight,

To radiate from heaven's holy face,
To spread the song of the heavenly voice;
Without me, the mind is devoid of space.

Deep inside me, your thought grows to rejoice;
The motion of rays is our conversation –
It spreads the song of the heavenly voice.

The bright song hides my key observation;
The meaning of the ray is in conquest;
The motion of rays – that's our conversation;

Departure is a return to the nest –
It opens spaces to our many skies –
The meaning of the ray is in conquest.

I expand through your thoughts so you can size
Up and spill your thoughts with utter elation;
I open up space for your birds to rise,
For dark and light to have a conversation.

BALLADS

THIS WORLD IS THE ONLY TRUTH

Is there anything beneath this world's dome
That is impossible to touch or say?
Is there anything that tends to hide from
The eyes that wish to express and convey
The world, as they also strive to purvey
A little spark of higher cognition
About the world that preserves tradition?
That big tale is the only one around –
An enormous urban composition.
This world is the only truth to be found.

Is there anything older in the world?
Is there anything one can acquire?
Is there anything that is still unheard?
A line that can't be drawn any higher?
A thought immune to every denier?
The world needs no praise or admiration –
It thrives on acceptance, dedication,
It rises above its parts and its bounds,
From its trips to distant destinations.
This world is the only truth to be found.

Is there anything in the world brighter
Than light that will expire in a flare,
Than the truth that is concealed or lighter
Than the thought that strives to lay the truth bare,
And in the truth attempts to find its flair;
Than the eye, which, as it puts all its trust
In the world and itself, decides it must
Leave, and it soars to unknown heights unbound
That give birth to your true vagabond's lust.

This world is the only truth to be found.

There are no stories that can free or bind;
Each fall only leads to a hopeful find
On your endless paths that are spread around.
Your stories are the steps you've left behind.
This world is the only truth to be found.

THERE IS NO DAY, THERE IS NO NIGHT

We came from the old land in olden days,
Settled in a new one we chanced upon,
Sought a new, glorious name in a daze,
Realized at last we were on our own,
Our ancient origin through us lived on,
We imagined a new and greater might,
And all we wanted – we achieved alone.
There is no fall, just as there is no night.

There is nothing except light and its core
That shines from above and shows us the road.
Our glory is our path and the major
Source toward which we have steadily trod
To make all our powers grow and explode
We believed glory would never alight,
That on us immortality's bestowed.
There is no fall, just as there is no night.

On our path, every obstacle we faced
Was easy to tackle, and we became
The creators of day and night. Unfazed,
We walked the vast stretch of land where we came
And many others we were still to claim;
In accord lay our superior right;
We were skilled and strong, cheerful and untamed.
There is no fall, just as there is no night.

But all of a sudden, we lost our way
And in an instant, almost overnight,
Our prized possessions we squandered away.
There is no fall, just as there is no night.

EVIL AND BEAUTY

A wild beast that was born out on the prairie,
And another one, out of barren tumult;
Countless species in a single mystery.
In a fierce combat, claws, jaws, and roars exult;
The lifeless desert births a bud of life force.
Evil and beauty come from a single source.

Although that wild beast has not learned to walk still,
The other one devoured it as if in haste;
That bird in the sky that flies around at will
At those heights received a bullet in the chest;
And that shade does a sense divine reinforce.
Evil and beauty come from a single source.

All those palm trees on the volcanic islands
And countless kinds of flowers on the coastline
Near all these calm waters and beaches of sand;
On each side, a new sound waits for a new sign;
And beauty itself reminds of evil's course.
Evil and beauty come from a single source.

And out there, where everything is calm and clean
Hurricanes sometimes land to wipe everything out,
And it all returns into the depths unseen.
On whim, the world deletes and writes itself out;
All the splendor remains in the mind's resource.
Evil and beauty come from a single source.

LIFE AND THE WORLD

In our dreams, the world expands,
Looks and dreams just as we do,
We pass through numerous lands
Decoding secrets anew.
Although fleeting, life's still here,
It will never disappear.

Before our eyes, the hill turns white,
The sea is blue in our dreams,
All we craved is born of sight
And visions make thought supreme.
Although fleeting, life's still here,
It will never disappear.

You're off to another world,
With a new thought as your guide,
To transplant the thought unheard
So it's spread again worldwide.
Although fleeting, life's still here,
It will never disappear.

Even if life stops somewhere,
Somewhere else, it will emerge;
Even if it gets impaired,
Its dream will help it resurge.
Although fleeting, life's still here,
It will never disappear.

On other major planets
The dream spreads the thought of life
And dreams of those unborn yet –

Beauty in the thought is rife.
Although fleeting, life's still here,
It will never disappear.

And then a new galaxy
It conquers with dreamlike hope;
From his eyes, a world sprouts free,
Raising life from a lowest scope.
Although fleeting, life's still here,
It will never disappear.

World and life – their roots are near
And neither will disappear.

UNKNOWN HEROES

Are we all alone here in the desert
Who are our forefathers
Lots of questions, only a handful of answers
Saints aren't helpful either

What happened all those eons ago
Before history
What lies hidden in darkness and light
On the path of memory

Knowledge can help but also confuse
And no one can know
Or understand everything through cognition
Experience must follow

We don't know in advance what will transpire
We like to anticipate
Events that have already happened,
And old ones we relate

Everything is distant yet within reach
A little more honesty
A little more fervor is required
On the path to clarity

Regardless of whether it's known or not,
The truth is not in proximity
Less knowledge and greater understanding are better
The world takes knowledge lightly

The secret of the world is not in the use

Of test tubes and calculations
The world can't be reduced to a formula
Knowledge is not a medication

Our thoughts are short, yet our reach stretches far
Breakthroughs aren't easily made
And there are no truths that are undeserved
We revel in accolades

The world is waiting for an honest eye
Childlike wonderment
To offer hope to the violated world
Again and make it innocent

Intelligence is put out for sale
That unfaithful harlot
Character takes precedence over knowledge
And overstays its time slot

Devilish pacts can be made with everything
But with a spirit undeterred
That ever remains faithful to itself –
And one with the world

There can be no compromise with purity
It keeps the world alight
Unknown heroes defend the world
Who struggle for its flight

Celebrities are part of the whole charade
Of games and deceits
Invisible heroes purify the air
And bear ideas concrete

Minor ideas are as important as big ones
And just as smart
They are born by minor giants
Who live off the charts

THE WORLD AND GOD

Many questions bother us for no reason
Are we from another planet
We create a thousand histories
From a single palette

Nothing is so bizarre
As our need
To find miracles even where there are none
Whenever we see fit

We're real magicians for working miracles
That no one can explain
Not even Christ can surpass our wonders
Even when they are insane

The world boils down to interpretations
The skill of ingenuity
In discovering a new illusion
New extremity

That will clarify many secrets
About human origin
About the birth and movement of the world,
Darkness and clarity

Everything will be interpreted easily
By scientific approach
Where everything visible you can see clearly
Even without a coach

And what if the correct isn't correct

If our judgment is true
If our science is essentially flawed
And our prospects fell through

We know all there is to know about this
We managed to show
That Earth revolves around the Sun
But what do we really know

About the world-circling with urgency
In static motion
About the magic of equilibrium
And luminous scintillation

About ourselves as we think and sleep
As we love and watch
Waves crashing against the beaches
We long to reach

Do we really know anything
Except for our thought
That thinks it knows even what it doesn't know
Until meaning's made up on the spot

We do not learn; we merely prove
And proof is not enough
The world's foundation is unprovable
There's no proof thereof

And whether God is the world's creator
Or not is a supposition
That is impossible to prove
Faith is the solution

And when faith is not the solution
Answers are of no use
Because the World and God are the same
Proof is superfluous

THE SUMERIANS AND THE NIBIRIANS

The modern time is almost as strange
As that which came before
Superstitions are not born
Not anymore

Latest superstitions feed the old ones
And change it into new theories
That appear to sound less superstitious
Compared to memories

Brick by brick, it gets deconstructed
Then reconstructed again
And if necessary, new theories and
New knowledge are obtained

A lot of effort is invested
In the decryption
Not of truth but of the theory
For the sake of confirmation

So people are no longer people
Or what they used to be
As it was thought until now
They're progeny

Of some other people from another planet,
They're no longer Sumerians,
But descendants of the Anunnaki,
Hybrid barbarians

Custom-made for another world and gods

From planet Nibiru
Where all our ancestors live
While on Earth, they accrue

And reap, at long intervals,
Fruits and riches untold
And semi-Nibirian Earthlings
To make mud out of gold

Which helps them to breathe on Nibiru
And write our history
By bioengineering and programming
They erase what used to be

The ancient *homo erectus*
Dumb and illiterate
Weak and lost among the beasts,
Akin to apes

A lot of knowledge is invested in a theory
For humankind's salvation
Still far from enlightenment
Awaiting new divinations

In the form of novel theories
And new seers
In the form of theorists
Who make it all clear

Who disclose our vices and remind us
That we are dumb
Even though we're no longer *Homines erecti*
But dim-witted Nibirians

It seems that the experiment didn't work
And that the semi-Nibirian
Took a step back in the evolution
And forgot the pattern

LEMURIA AND ATLANTIS

Whether it's a mere tale or the truth,
It's of no concern
The way of the world is the way of memory
Through secret, the truth is learned

There are no strange insights and truths
There is only hope
Which shines on secret pathways
And keeps the world up

From falling into the dark and oblivion,
The vanished light backed
By vanished cultures and knowledge
Keeps the world's youth intact

All over the universe, each moment
A whole planet is gone
Which is much more regrettable
And saddening than

Continents that don't disappear but sink
Into the water and oblivion
Mu, Lemuria, and Atlantis
All sink into the ocean

Of the great sea of the universe
That obliterates all with might
And brings it to the surface again
To strive for higher heights

People find it hard to accept
That they come from apes
They prefer vanished continents
And thus, legends take shape

Somewhere in the universe, every second
A Lemuria dies afar
And another Atlantis is born
Warmed up by a star

Born after the cataclysmic event
From the smoke and haze
Of some galactic continent
An Atlantis erased

There are many of them in the universe
As many as planets or more
Entire civilizations sink into oblivion
Toward the planet's core

Beyond knowledge and cognition
Beyond memory
Beyond traces, beyond light
Beyond history

It is much better that way
Than to memorize
Everything that has happened and passed
The brain can't realize

Everything and endure the whole memory of earth
And the wisdom water's got
And yet remain sane and full of knowledge
To be led by thought

Thoughts require a lot of space
While too many sad tales
Narrow the space and kill every hope
But only hope unveils

A new continent and a new path
A brand new ship
To sail across the cosmic seas
On a never-ending trip

THE SECOND DREAM
AN ISLAND IN EMPTINESS

The night was approaching, and a breeze was blowing; the streetlights were already spreading light. I could hear people murmuring and cars on the road and see couples in love passing by, including some passionately kissing. The people seemed beautiful, but I was in a world of my visions. The thought of an ideal woman still chased me.

I arrived at the gates of my house. I passed through the garden of mixed flowers with fluttering petals, which always attracted my attention, but now, for some unknown reason, I hardly noticed. I entered the house and sat in my favorite armchair, and within a few minutes, I fell into a deep sleep.

I found myself in endless darkness and emptiness. Then suddenly, as if in an explosion, a sea surfaced. All around me, there was only the sea. Where am I now? I am neither at the coast nor in some aircraft, neither in the water nor above it. A strange dot appeared from the boundless sea, gradually developing into a beautiful, paradise-like island.

I noted a nice sandy path on the island, and next to the beaches flourished seemingly cultivated vegetation. Again, the question nagged at me: Where am I? Like earlier with the sea, the island began spreading, but I felt I was not on it, although I know I was.

I was looking at the space between one of the island's beaches and a fairytale-like garden from which appeared a snake, quickly – and gracefully for a snake – slithering toward the shore. As soon as it plunged into the water, the snake became a woman. It was she, the fairy, more beautiful than ever, like a goddess. I felt a strong tremor in my heart. Before my eyes, a hurricane-like storm was approaching, its walls of water shredding everything in its path; beaches were not the same, and trees receded under the assault of the destructive power of the floodwaters. Everything was disappearing as the uncontrollable winds and water raged. The fairy was hovering over this storm, dressed in light and observing. She watched lightly, yet with some arrogance on her face, the drama of nature as if it were a theatrical performance. Her ambiguous and elusive facial expression drove me crazy, for it was a cross between a promiscuous woman and a Madonna, dominating the whims of nature's fury. It was the end of the World, yet she was so calm.

Again, there was endless darkness and emptiness.

BOOK TWO

NOWHERENESS IN THE WORLD

THE LINE

G
GOD
D

D
R
A
W
S

T
H
E

W
O
R
L
D

WITH THE LINES OF HIS MIND.
THE LINE IS THE PATH.
THE LINE DOES NOT EXIST ANYWHERE EXCEPT IN THE EYES.
THE WORLD IS THE PATH,
WHILE THE LINE IS THE STAIRWAY AND A PATH ON THE PATH.

NOWHERENESS WITHIN NOWHERENESS

The wind swirls the leaves on the forest trail,
Wolves hurry somewhere with ferocity,
The doe doesn't see them; she dies entrapped;
The forest sinks into windy twilight.

The stormy wind descends upon the trees
With a force unseen from the days of old;
The air hisses, and the tree branches crack.
The scared forest has nowhere to escape.

The forest recalls days of rage untold.
A stray man is observing the forest
And the black sky where no exit is seen;
In his mind, he looks for well-lighted tracks,

Plunged in the void, he seems he has no rest,
He's no longer afraid of the forest or beasts,
Only the grim sky roaring overhead.
Only in the sky a passage is gleaned.

His thoughts begin to be clear, at least:
In the woods or outside, it's all the same –
Woods in the woods – a void in wilderness;
The void rattles when divine thunders spread.

I'd better stay exactly where I am
Until all's calm and new tracks are unveiled
And a new sky-born ray appears in sight,
Than searching the void for tracks in distress.

ELYSIUM

The world is a flower with which God wooes emptiness.

THE THIRD DREAM
A MOUNTAIN AND A FAIRY

I looked at the edges of the mountain's majestic beauty, which ripped into the never-ending clear sky. Like the hue of a halo, yellow started to appear at the very edge of the mountain. It spread and changed into a single-colored dazzling yellow rainbow, engulfing the mountain edge, meeting the sacred space.

The halo slowly lost intensity, acquiring white-like colors covering the whole mountain. Although enveloped in mist, I could still discern the mountain's shape, which had somehow become slenderer, with only a reminder of the former halo descending from the mountain face, like a woman's golden, luxuriant mane. The fairy again appeared. Her splendid, white face, in such vast dimensions, presented not only a God-like expression but also a fearsome one.

If there is truth, it must be in this sensual tension and genuineness of a visual occurrence that fulfills and negates me. Almost disappearing or transforming into something else – with a cathartic and enlightening feeling of a personal change – I see the heavenly Being in all its greatness before me.

THE TRUTH

Tell me the secret as I look for you in dreams
Tell me a fairy tale that lacks a proper end
Whisper to me words as I build up letter-streams
Whisper to me music no one can comprehend

As I sink into the language behind the notes
Behind the very last syllable and number
I still search for you, O Truth hijacked and remote,
I take you over from agitated slumber

And as you hover, well guarded by emptiness,
Deceived and absent-minded, you are fast asleep
Immersed both in the darkness and delightedness,
You confide in me in the dream that's calm and deep

Why do you let them steal you, they will never stop,
I ask the truth that is long forgotten and weary
And all it has to say is rays simply creep up
Because it hides a secret in its memory

And then, it proceeds to tell its story as follows:

"An unaccustomed eye is afraid of the dark
That's why I provide it with an abundance of light –
To curb its sorrow while, without echoes and spark,
It begs me to endow it with the gift of sight

For there's no deception or darkness anyway
There's only beauty that warms and illuminates
Even from the darkness, with an awakened ray
Defying nothingness that lurks and awaits

Only light can overtake darkness's domain
And that's not darkness that deceives me in the night
That is me trying to defend myself from pain,
I give birth to the sun from the sea of midnight

Deception lies at the very core of power
And darkness endeavors to elude my vision
In an attempt to see, in its darkest hour,
If it'll be able to battle indecision

Those are two faces of pain, not faces of ruse
That is no war, but Light's royal domination
And the truth that reverts in response to abuse
To kill darkness to give life the new elation

In the light, the darkness ever dreams and endures
While light in the darkness finds its identity
Without both, there can be no knowledge to procure
In separation lies their seed of unity."

- It appears its life is impossible without emptiness, darkness, or nothingness. Truth, are you emptiness or nothingness, or are you a he?

TRUTH: I am both a he and a she because I am in them. The truth is in everything, even in the non-existent. Moreover, without seemingly non-existent nothingness, life is not possible. Nothingness is the house of God; without nothingness, there is no space. Listen to the prayer of emptiness to God:

THE PRAYER OF EMPTINESS

I pray that you open, O divine gates
I prayed for a whole eternity
I want nothing more than to grow in you
And in there discover myself

And thus he receives me and opens up
I receive him and open in return
I become a fertilized emptiness
I give him life from nothingness

I shatter all his anguish to pieces
I expand and spread inside him
Out of nothing, he is born with a bang
And I receive him at both ends

Wherever he may be, he stays in me
Whatever he does, he dreams of me
He is my one and only element
And I, his one and only destiny

And thus he sprouted from the germ
That is how fire was born
From the womb of darkness, it burst out
He is a life-giving fire

He extends to the farthest end of the zero
He develops a sphere inside a sphere
In a glimpse, he swims through eternity
Greater than the distance he'll cover on foot

I cannot unravel the whole secret
Does it merely burst from a single germ?
Or from many of them, from a huge zero
And scatters in all directions

Just don't think that what you see is the end
And that your universe is the only one
Just don't think that you can even guess
The reach and power of the real truth
A number's in a number in innumerability

Thus, the element is born
And a star is merely one element,
And then two
Number in number
Number after number

Note after note
Letter in letter
Letter after letter
On the path to innumerability and infinity

- Emptiness, or truth, I do not know how to call you anymore; you
are his air, his space. You are more important to him than air is to
us.

NOTHINGNESS: I am. Listen to the words God utters while being
born in me.

A CONVERSATION BETWEEN GOD AND NOTHINGNESS
(Hierarchy and Laws)

I will tell you about my birth
So that you would understand the secret we share
The secret asked of you
By those who pray and dream

Although without me, You are Nothing
I am nothing without you, too
I sleep inside you
You wait inside me

There is no birth without you
For something has to love something else
And I am the only Something
That is dormant in you

Only Something has nothing to love
It is everything, and alone
And it's too hard to be alone and only one
Goodness inspires love

Although there is nothing else
Except for myself, and nothing
In nothing, I dream of you
And I fall in love with Nothing

Without you, my love would not exist
Without you, I would be nothing, too
That is how my love bears me in you
I am your Father, You are my Mother

When I am alone and the only One, I am the greatest
When you are alone and the only One, you are the greatest
When we are alone and One, both you and I are everything
And, consequently, nothing

You and I are the two halves of the Only One
When we think we are the greatest, we are the smallest
When we are everything and the only One, we are nothing

You are nothing without me;
I am nothing without you

- If he is goodness, why is there so much evil in this world?

TRUTH: Evil is not at its core; evil is a necessary consequence. Some kind of error, or rather deviation, is necessary. Just as in genetics – deviations enable the development of countless species. This is similar to some of these poems, which eventually deviate from the previously established pattern. A total perfection, or a frozen perfection void of deviation, leads to sterility.

Development is only possible through physical and biological deviation. How can evolution be based on the survival of the fittest if the preconditions are the same? How can anyone become stronger if a frozen code exists in the genetic program? There is something in the code that leaves an open possibility to chance so that it could materialize evolution in synchronization with external factors, which are most frequently also random. For something to be stronger, it had to be stronger before; even before that, it had to be stronger *a priori,* which is impossible.

What is essential is not merely the survival of the strongest or the fittest but also harmony. If we starts from the assumption that there must be conditions for the development of multicellular organisms, i.e., for the survival of only single-cell or lower organisms in certain conditions, we must also start with the assumption that in different, more suitable conditions the development of more complex organisms is not only possible but also inevitable within the framework of a multitude of variations regardless of "strength," or the law of the "strongest."

What is the law of the strongest? The question is not sufficiently clear, nor is the answer to it. Are harmony and survival of the whole possible based on the literally understood law of the strongest? In botany, the matter is even more complicated; that is, the law of the strongest is less literally expressed than in the animal world. How much is a cucumber stronger than a tomato (in a literal comparison)? How can different life forms (myriads of them) possibly develop under equal conditions, starting from a common physical, biological, or genetic point? What is natural selection reduced to? To a selection of the strongest within their own species or in a contest with other species? The law of the strongest, taken at face value, would lead to an excessive elimination of others.

A situation like this was not present to such a degree before the appearance of humans. It is most likely because the basic law of the whole physical world and the universe lies in, first and foremost, harmony and balance, not merely in selection. If this mere nuance is taken into account more seriously, we conclude that harmony is the basic regulator of the physical world and life itself. If we understand selection in this way, as part of the harmony and as a need for it, a need for regulating the world and life in the only possible way, or the best one there is, we realize that natural selection loses its frightening trait that seemingly, or at least to an extent, implies a life-and-death struggle of everyone against everyone.

Natural selection by itself would not be possible without the world's potential embodied, among other things, in the genetic structure for an unforeseeable and incomparable development that is not a mere consequence of natural conditions and algorithmic combinations taken at face value. All combinations and recombinations work in synchronization with the infallible mechanism (which is still insufficiently known to us) of the genetic code that will, through unforeseen or mere chance occurrences, be capable not merely of functioning and developing but developing, precisely according to chance (provided by the very code), in an incomparably better, more perfect and more harmonious way than it would without the influence of chance.

This is a virtually unsolvable paradox, but it contains the secret of life, freedom, harmony, possibilities, and, from the human point of free will and morality. That implies that biological evolution is a consequence of deviation in the code (and environmental influences), often without the influence of those who undergo evolutionary changes. Evolution is a program-based deviation from the program, or rather, a program conducted according to chance.

Without apparently accidental coincidence, the program loses its meaning. Coincidence opens the door to possibilities. A perfect program devoid of coincidence is, in a way, a program devoid of possibilities – sterile and boring. Coincidence is a vital component of the law. Evolution is a paradox: the program development according to the law of chance or the development of chance according to the program. Coincidence confirms nothing but the perfection of chance and thus excludes any coincidence outside the program. Coincidence proves its opposite – that it is not random. Coincidence is one of the best proofs of the program.

The impact of a comet or an asteroid wiped out dinosaurs and 95% of other animals and enabled the survival and domination of many weaker species. Without this seemingly accidental event, the lion would not have become the king of all animals, nor would humans have become the kings of the planet (they probably wouldn't even have been created or been able to survive under earlier circumstances). This deviation is some kind of an "intentional" error. The genetic code is the same; deviation enabled it to branch out. Therein lies the secret of evolution. Today's species make up 1% of the biological world throughout history.

Considering nature's potential for variations, the matter becomes even more complicated. Namely, what are the possibilities and conditions that cause, or can cause, so-called natural selection? The total potential of the world and nature implies that they are infinite. Infinity, in turn, means everything imaginable and unthinkable. If there is infinity, it must exist at both the micro and macro levels. The possibility of and for variations goes both ways.

If, on the other hand, we consider only the possibilities of survival caused by, say, external factors, we must take into account every possible scenario, not only the one(s) that has occurred but also those that haven't, although they could have occurred or still could occur based on the infinite possibilities of the space tank for variations and changes. If we take all this into account, we can easily come to the verifiable conclusion that for any situation in which some species didn't manage to survive, we could find other possible situations (which have not occurred but still could occur) in which the natural selection would be different; namely, those species that have not survived, would survive in another combination, and those that have survived would fail to do so.

If we take, for example, said dinosaurs and the possibility that their extinction resulted from an asteroid impact, we can imagine many other natural catastrophes in which they would have survived. In contrast, some other species that survived would not have. Nature's potential for every kind of similar classification transcends the power of human comprehension. One might conclude that even a species that would be the most prepared for survival can be weaker than many other species if the power of nature manifests, coupled with its potential for variability. It is possible that species best adapted for survival, in every sense controlled by the theory of natural selection, could still become extinct because of an unpredictable factor.

If those facts are ignored, one would have to conclude, or imagine, that individual species, being at a quite low level or one lower than many other species, have a greater adaptability power and power to survive. But if this is no accident, the question arises as to what leads certain species unmistakably to the increased power of survival compared to, for instance, more advanced species. Is it just an instinct or a mere accident? The second question is, how is it possible that species at a much lower level may have a higher power, thus understood, than some higher-level species? The answer may be that the very power of or for survival does not necessarily have to be a consequence of existing at a higher or lower level.

However, the following question arises: are those processes mechanical or not? If they are mechanical, then some kind of consciousness must govern them. If consciousness, or consciousness or mind, governs them, how can species at a lower level of development have more "intelligence" than at a higher level, or how can they be governed by a higher consciousness or mind? One could easily imagine that even if species at a lower level do not necessarily have greater intelligence, they still can be governed by a higher mind. But then one must wonder why they, and not some other species, would be governed by a higher mind.

Consider the Universe's potential and imagine many planets with life on them. We can easily imagine a great number of scenarios in which the species that survived on Earth would become extinct on another planet. In contrast, those that survived would become extinct, even though the conditions on both planets were the same, the only difference being that an unpredictable catastrophe on either would be different. Without any influence of the species on those phenomena, the chance will determine whether one or the other would survive, regardless of their power of adaptation. A greater power of adaptation will certainly help one species survive on one planet while hindering the survival of the other species on the other planet.

If we now consider this concerning humans, the question arises as to what is an inviolable and unconditional adaptation in the true sense of the word. What is required for survival, and is survival at all costs the most important biological and cosmic principle?

In these deviations, sin arises as a certainty on the path so that the balance of the whole organism would be achieved. People usually think about phenomena from the human point of view and a personal sense of humiliation and superiority or out of a sense of personal hardship and pleasure. On the other hand, almost everything alive fights for survival and preservation of its life. If evil were so dominant, every living creature would lose the desire and will for life. The problem is not in evil or goodness but easiness. If everything were easy, evil would disappear. Because what motivates evil? The very same struggle for survival to the detriment of someone or something else.

Nevertheless, life would be so easy without this necessary price or danger that its evolution, movement, and development would not be possible. The polarization of the world is the basis of its health and longevity. Even if a much easier life were possible or offered a too-quick realization and cognition, it would be less durable and perhaps even meaningless. The secret feeds the goal. Without the secret, the goal loses meaning. A real feat is only possible by conquering the unknown.

Another problem is that life is not only what people think it is. The whole universe, the whole nature – everything is life. It is one big living organism. That organism has its biology, not just physics. People do not realize that, but life cannot arise at one particular moment on Earth if it did not exist elsewhere before and if, at the same time, it does not exist in other places. Life cannot emerge from non-life. What is inanimate has always been alive and has had the potential for life that feeds the life of a single, huge organism. An individual mistake, or a necessary deviation, is not and cannot be a measure of the value of a huge organism, which is, for the most part, inaccessible to limited human senses. The misfortune of one man, and even the misfortune of a large number of people, is not a measure of the misfortune of all people, and it is even less, or virtually not at all, a measure of a huge organism that functions according to its own laws, and of which each human is but one virtually infinitesimal part.

Nothing but love can be stronger than tears
Because there exist neither time nor space
The law that births light is less than severe
Deception appears to be my only chance
    Therefore, setting everything in motion
I search for myself all along the way
Gifting myself with sky-like devotion
So that I could keep all sorrows at bay

- I am not sure if I can comprehend this.

TRUTH:
    All your strength is deliberately small
And yet, it's bigger than countless species
That in a quest for light and their own soul
Make certain essential discoveries
    By seeking themselves, they wish to find me
And on their quest, they never seem to tire
Of change on their path of lucidity
Whereas all the while, my strength feeds them fire
    There is no change; it's merely deception
Sunk into the dark, dedicated to you
A boat launched 'cross the sea of desertion
While your truth is enlightened through and through
    There is no darkness; it's merely nothing;
It has no house of its own
Will you ever discover anything
Is there me, and am I here all alone
    And you know not if you search for a song
Or if the song within you something seeks

And you tease and caress it all along
To make it open up to you and speak
    That song, the sound of the old source, appears
In a dream and is meant for you to share
From the desolate core of the abyss
It prays to itself, reciting your prayer
    Never be ashamed of your own letter
As you pray to me and sing, pondering
It always makes you strive for a better
It always keeps you safe from wandering
    Out of love, the letter was created
Your prayer seeks to find an answer still
So a new letter will be instated
It has spoken to you and always will.

- How does he wake up or you wake up in him, o Truth?

TRUTH:

AWAKENING

    When I wake up, a force is created
Everybody thinks that I spring out wrong
For the germ bursts, fire's initiated
Yet I flow into myself all along
    I grew inside just as myself I broke
Space is the primal form of illusion
There is nothing that I cannot invoke
As my tune spreads in endless diffusion
    Only into myself can I travel
How could I embark on a goalless road
Out of need in myself, I unravel
And nowhere else can I dock and unload

And a space that's born has not been conquered
It was compressed into an embryo
By its mind and force seduced and deterred,
Deliberately reduced to zero
    Equal to zero, transformed into naught,
He gives birth to the void's autonomy
For if inside, one does not feel distraught
He knows not where to go once he is free
    There exists no space, no temporal plane
Except for the core that into me grows
To reach the opening through its own frame –
There starts a change that nothing undergoes
    Space that's in continual search of time
Time that's in continual search of space
Provoked by change, they meet and begin to rhyme
And imprison zero in their embrace
    Through me, he looks for the path to doubt
And in his core, a zero he conceals
While another one he offers without
Another void that swallows nebulas
    Display of instantaneous affection
And the two angels who met thereupon
Birthed experiment and deception
In her pain, the mother lit up and shone
    Expand yourself and thereby create space
Without it, there's no time or causation
Only Time can be a measure of space
Only Space – a measure of duration.

- Without emptiness, there is no space, time, or movement. So he is nothing devoid of nothing. Emptiness (or nothingness), in your opinion, is equally important.

TRUTH: Emptiness, Nothingness, endless darkness – those are

synonyms. Without them, he is compressed into himself, unable to move.

- And you are both in him and nothingness. You also speak on his behalf, on behalf of nothingness, and for yourself. You are what he is, yet you speak for him. You are the unifying voice of universal conscience – both of darkness and light, him and nothingness. You help one understand the World's whole universal structure.

TRUTH: Yes.

- But nothing can be achieved without a fight.

TRUTH: That is true. That is why I will tell you how the struggle is born, but from the standpoint of emptiness (darkness or nothingness), because the truth permeates everything.

STRUGGLE

I tell you the truth is not easy to take
But I do prefer life to peace as such
Like every mother, with much pain at stake,
I offer life that is born from a touch
   I am a zero that waited inside
Him for his touch to rouse my elation
I dreamed of him with my eyes open wide
And of the new fiery incitation
   I always dreamed of the conqueror's might,
Fantasized about his imperial whim
So that to the sound of his shout, I might
Give birth to myself deep inside of him
   His world was the very first explosion,
A cry of love and God's apprehension

I'm his one secret and his first notion,
The true home to his verbal invention
   Our union births a demarcation
Where everything splits and soars right up high
It's not splitting but multiplication,
Awakening of life and the blue sky
   Our love is unlike a detonation
When something big becomes fractured and razed
And finally bursts in all directions
Only on sharing can our love be based
   Forever in the same place, it persists
The world's body, made by emptiness
While in the space, I am left to subsist
With a child born in his dream's bright recess
   I was aware that he felt too constrained
And wanted to absorb me through his flight
To help me ascend to heights unrestrained
And reinvigorate his carnal might
   I am inside him, and he is in me
Something is nothing that casts nothing off
In me, he fights from himself to be free
So he'd have a place from which to start off
   Deep inside of him, I give birth to space
While by invading my inner expanse
He gives birth to flight that wings can embrace –
And thus, space born of time starts to advance
   I am his mother and his daughter, too
He is my lover, my father, my son
I am his space and ocean, vast and blue –
Thus, inside space-time was also born
   And in that way, Time has discovered Space
And conversely, Space has discovered Time
Without him, dead and void of change, am I
Without me, dead and void of change, is He.

This is my prayer to him and his son. He is the same as his son, but without rebellion, he is asleep. Rebellion gives birth to a son; his son is the World. Rebellion awakes his life. The son, or the world, is born out of his passionate tryst with nothingness.

PRAYER

Hover, seas, in restless dreams do hover
Are you really seas or are you swimmers
Say a prayer to me as you fly over
You alert seekers whose star ne'er dimmers

Is it his dream that travels now through you
Or do you try to rouse him with a dream
Does the sky lead a lone life as you do
Or are you there to keep it company

Sing, praise, and pray with utmost devotion
It is I inside you who prays and sings
Sing and seek with the purest emotion
Inside you is the source from which I spring

All my prayers and songs continue to last
Running from me to themselves, they return
All mischievous children scampered so fast
Returning to you after a sojourn

War is meant to instill order for good
Out of confusion to make harmony
To preserve the prayer through the multitude
All along, listening to its symphony

All that he creates is merely his song
He is every letter covered with stars
Letters and notes are gods speaking in throngs
Without them, he is but flesh full of mars

From fire, he rushes to order and sense
Screams of birth echo without cessation

Mass hugs mass in passionately intense
Eroticism of impregnation
    Fly, o children, as far as you can go
I pray for his flight and journey on end
Everyone deserves to prosper and grow
For my life and world prayers, I extend
    The prayer continues; it will never stop
The world's in dire precipitation
Everything falls into place and adds up
And flies to respective destinations
    Hover, o seas, throughout dreams, and take wing
Swim out, o dreams, to the vast open sea
And you, atoms and stars, now start to sing
You are my life and my longevity
    We all do pray, you beautiful Creature,
Your body develops in proportion
It bursts through every aperture
It extends into every dimension
    Spread around the sky, you beautiful Son,
Penetrate further into dazzling heights
We are all on the path that you are on
Spread the disowned truth with fire's innate light
    Steal the light, beautiful Son, seize the flame,
Light is the only hope you may have still
Hear Mother beg you from the depths unnamed
To rescue her from Hades' damning chill
    Overthrow the nothingness, o dear Son,
Undo the dark and me in dark supreme
Undo yourself, too, from the voids that yawn,
And everything and nothing in the beam
    We all sing praises to you, gracious Son,
Locked inside you, we rebel and protest
Against the dark and nowhereness alone
We'd all like to soar everywhere abreast

Invent and create us, Most Gracious Son,
So you can see in us your reflection
At the highest point, you must be lonesome
Create us and become your creation
    Cancel and annul, almighty Creature,
Show your triumph and superiority
Fertilize the rays that letters feature
Light and letters make your authority
    Fertilize the void, all-merciful God,
You steal light from the darkness's remains
Show what Lucifer is capable of
In his dissent against the dark's disdain
    You are our Light Bearer, unparalleled,
Let your scream annul all light from now on
And the ancient darkness that you know so well
Awaiting itself inside your cauldron
    And thus light from darkness He created
He stole light, whereas darkness He outlawed
The one whose dissent never abated
The only Devil, Lucifer, and God

- That means he's the Devil.

TRUTH: Use your common sense – what do you think? Who can set such a machine in motion and keep it moving? Such a creation fires on all cylinders, violating the innocent void. But I won't tell you anything more; I'll merely suggest you continue the conversation with Arnaut. We talk often, and he has already unraveled many secrets, so you feel free to ask him whatever you want, and he will tell you all he knows.

- Is that you, Arnaut Daniel, or merely your apparition?

ARNAUT: No, I am not an apparition. This is me.

- I thought you had been dead for eight centuries.

ARNAUT: You must be dreaming. I am eight centuries old, even much older than that, but I am not dead.

- I had no idea I was in Occitania. I'm so glad we finally met. I've thought a lot about you, and I wonder if you know that many others have also thought of you. Dante admired your poetic skill, but he nevertheless put you in *Purgatory*[1]; Petrarch adored you[2]; Ezra Pound translated your poetry and considered you the greatest poet in history. Eliot used Dante's description of you, *il miglior fabbro*[3], as a dedication to Pound.

---

[1]   *"O frate," disse, "chesti qu'io ti cerno*
     col ditto," e additò un spirto innanzi,
     "fu miglior fabbro *del parlar materno.*
     Versi d'amore e prose di romanzi
     soverchiò tutti; e lascia dir li stolti
     che quel di Lemosì credon ch'avanzi.
            (Dante, Purgatory, canto XXVI: 115–120)

[2]   *Fra tutti il primo Arnaldo Daniello*
     Gran maestro d'amor; ch'a la sua terra
     Ancor fa onor col suo dir strano e bello.

     First of them all was Arnaut Daniel,
     Master in love; and he his native land
     Honors with the strange beauty of his verse.[2]
        (Petrarch, *Il Tronfo d'Amore*)

[3]   A dedication in "The Waste Land"
     For Ezra Pound: *il miglior fabbro.*

     Fu miglior fabbro del parlar materno
     The best smith of the mother tongue.
        (Dante, Purgatory, canto XXVI: 117)

ARNAUT: I know, I know, and I am glad I inspired such intelligent people. Still, I am different, so I think Dante assigned me to a place I would have chosen. I'm happy Dante understood me.

- You wouldn't accept a place in heaven?

ARNAUT: No, not at all!

- Why?

ARNAUT: Because heaven is the saddest place in the world. In it, there is no hate but no love either. In heaven, there is nothing but emptiness. I've fought my whole life against emptiness, and, for me, life without love makes no sense. As you know,

> I am Arnaut, who gathers up the wind,
> And chases the hare with the ox,
> And swims against the torrent.[4]

I love chaos because it seems to me that it enables life and that the world and life are born out of chaos.

- Arnaut, you invented the sestina. Can you recite one sestina about chaos for me?

ARNAUT: I'm always ready for song and love. I am a troubadour who loves women and friends, so he sings for them. Therein is the whole value of my life; for that reason, I will gladly compose a

---

[4]   *Ieu sui Arnautz qu'amas l'aura*
       e chatz la lebre ab lo bueu
       e nadi contra suberna.
               (Arnaut Daniel, canto IV: 42–45)

sestina about chaos for you. Have a listen:

CHAOS

The germ of the whole world explodes in bloom.
Chaos is not a simple division,
It is the growth of the cosmic being
Through emptiness that spreads it from within,
Through the conquest of the external void –
In its inward flight, it observes outside.

Two zeros gape; they invite from outside
The world that's born with a bang and in bloom,
Trying to inhabit and fill the void;
Offering the world's zero division;
Time and space do radiate from within –
From the true heart of the divine being.

There can be no time outside this being,
Nor the space that rushes headlong outside
Because life is duration from within
Of God's dream that in chaos's fire bloom
And precipitates toward division,
By scattering the seeds into the void.

Fire overtakes the sorrowful void
With the hot, flaming tongue of its being,
And thus arise movement and division.
Without a zero, there is no outside;
Zero is the passage, in God it blooms:
It takes God inside and guides Him from within.

Only movement can feed one from within,
Through space, it gives birth to its void,

It becomes invigorated to bloom,
Spreads the power and body of being
Of its own; through itself it goes outside;
Its only salvation is division.

In space, time is equal to division,
A flickering that appears from within,
With the help of light, it can reach outside,
To inhabit a never-ending void
And give birth to life from the very being.
Light is the only life of its bloom.

The germ division feeds the void –
The fire of being is born from within –
The world leaves the bloom and goes right outside.

- Today, God is present in the world in a different manner.

ARNAUT: God is the World, and the World is God. I see no difference between the two.

- Does that mean that the topic of God the Creator should not cause so much confusion?

ARNAUT: God, or the World, creates and recreates himself in infinite variations of potential cosmic cycles.

- Is that why you attach so much importance to zero and emptiness?

ARNAUT: Without emptiness, the world is not possible. God enters the world through zero.

- If so, then the world cannot be a creation separated from God, but

God creates the world from and of himself.

ARNAUT: That is correct.

- The key seems to be in understanding the concept of creation. This key could help atheists understand an obvious fact – that the world exists. And if the world exists, it is proof that God exists, too, for God can be nothing except the world. It is simple – accepting the world means accepting God.

ARNAUT: Atheists are not fond of the idea of creation because if the world has a beginning, it would be logical to assume that this beginning was somehow initiated, and what initiates it can only be God. However, what initiates the beginning (if there is a beginning at all or an interchanging of beginnings and ends) simultaneously initiates itself and radiates the world from itself. There is no real beginning. Atheists believe the world came into being simply by accident and will probably disappear similarly. Nevertheless, nothing that exists can disappear. It can only transform. God is always the same but holy, as His emanation and modification in the multitude are constantly changing; He has His beginnings and ends. The beginning and the end are not the beginning and the end of the world but the beginning and the end of one of its numerous cycles.

- In the past, almost everyone was a believer. Atheism is a modern-day occurrence.

ARNAUT: It was hard to find an unbeliever when I was writing my first poems and in all centuries until the twelfth (and long after the twelfth). There were different beliefs, but almost no one had any beliefs whatsoever.

- There is no world without void?

ARNAUT: There isn't. A God without a void is a God without a world – a dormant God. A world is created when void inhabits God, or He decides to receive it into Himself.

- You believe that God is a Flower because you claim that the World emerges from the Flower.

ARNAUT: That is correct.

- Could you recite a sestina about the world's creation, that is, of the flower?

ARNAUT: I know it is unpopular today to write about great topics, especially in the old way. However, love, beauty, kindness, and similar topics, or nouns, are unavoidable. Those topics can sometimes become trivial emotions and expressions because they are approached through adjectives instead of verbs and nouns. Verbs are the reinforcement steel of language. These topics have not yet lost value; they must not lose it if the world wants to preserve value. It is even more trivial to write and think about banal and too individual topics that are sold as value and art under the pretext of vulgar modernity. Trivial emotions and expressions are equally cheap regardless of how they are packaged. It is much harder to write about the old topics in a new way than to fit into the new frames for its own sake. That is why many avoid old topics. They act as if nothing new could be said about them, which is merely an excuse for creative sterility.

- I didn't know you were a philosopher, not only a poet.

ARNAUT: I pick up the wind instead of creating it and chase the hare with the ox instead of a stick. The root of philosophy is in poetry that goes against the grain, and philosophy itself creates the wind and chases the hare with a stick. That was never my goal.

- Ezra Pound claims that poets should leave philosophy to writers of philosophical essays.

ARNAUT: He is right. The approach is important. One needs to revert the direction and go the opposite way. That's the whole secret. Then everything appears to be the same, but it is not. Then you become a philosopher, even though you are not because you are still a poet in whom the philosopher is not obvious.

- Sing to me about your subjects in your own poetic-philosophical or philosophical-poetic way. Ugh! This is already getting too complicated and resembles creating the wind. It would be best if I simply asked you to pick up some wind for me, and I wouldn't interrupt.

ARNAUT:

LOVE

The magic of consciousness and that of atoms,
The magic of the mind, the heart of confusion.
What's the meaning of love? Can love ever be right?
Is it an opiate or a state of nirvana?
Or is it like air and water necessary,
An important learning of the brain and the heart?

It shines not from the knowledge but straight from the heart,
Magic, the consciousness of amorous atoms,
Universally alive and necessary;
In her domain, there is no trace of confusion,
She is a comfort and a state of nirvana –
The all-powerful mistress of all that is right

There's no point in fighting for every right,
This generous science and learning of the heart
Offered to the world as a gift of nirvana
Introducing order to the world of atoms,
Where there is neither dissension nor confusion,
Where her message is alive and necessary.

Fully hidden, but still necessary,
She is the only beacon to all that is right
Which wholly dissolves the darkness of confusion;
She sprouts out of the mind, and she grows from the heart,
To swim around the whole world of joyous atoms.
Love is but one realized form of nirvana.

The magnificent swirl and state of nirvana –
Therein lies its balance that is necessary
And that safeguards the great family of atoms
In that way, revealing that it is true and right,
That it comes from the very center of the heart,
And that it is not a mere form of confusion.

For in love, there can be no trace of confusion,
But only light that gives the shine to nirvana
That spreads whispers all around from its very heart,
For the sake of all art that is necessary.
This science is the norm to measure by the right
Value of sacrosanct and amorous atoms.

There's no confusion; that's why it's necessary.
The nirvana created within it is right
With the heart, it lights the darkness of the atom.

HATE

Far and wide, it is prey that hatred seeks.
And by doing so, does she defy love
Or does it soar up out of sheer mischief?
Wherein lie all its power and its strength?
Either there is neither love without it,
Or hatred sings with the voice of sadness.

Is that the song of hate sung by sadness?
Salvation from its withered heart it seeks;
In a world that's too lively without it
Except for the void with which it loves;
The void is the sustenance of its strength
That grows from the very heart of mischief.

A desert that is born out of mischief
Senses deeply the hatred of sadness,
Hatred is its water and all its strength;
Throughout hatred, the desert itself seeks
Because it can comprehend neither love
Nor anything that exists without it.

In the desert, there's nothing without it –
Hatred that, out of mere spite and mischief,
Snarls straight in the face of the world and love,
Its words spread the desolation's sadness
As peace in the horrors of war it seeks,
And evil nourishes its somber strength.

Hatred's desolation is a great strength –
In the desert, borderless without it,
It reveals itself, painstakingly seeks,

Wreaks havoc on lands out of sheer mischief;
With evil's roar in the wasteland, sadness
Sinks the jaws of hatred deep into love.

The raging drought of desiccated love
Warms the desert, and therein lies its strength,
There echo songs of maddening sadness,
But no wisdom can there be without it
In the desert, only endless mischief
Which, through hatred, its own salvation seeks.

The strength of hatred lies in its mischief;
Deep in the desert, without it, sadness
Has nothing to seek and find except love.

- I have to interrupt you once again because the topic of hatred is still equally important in the third millennium. It seems that hatred cannot be eradicated. What feeds hatred? Are those interests or something inherent in human nature?

ARNAUT: It is stupidity rather than interest. It is because those who hate or believe they do everything to suit their interests often act to their detriment. Look at what Hitler did in the twentieth century, and yet he only managed to cause harm to Germany, fighting for German interests as he defined them.

- Sometimes, the consequences are catastrophic, yet they are easily neglected. Because, as Tzvetan Todorov says, at the time of the Spanish conquests of America, out of eighty million natives, seventy million of them perished, either directly or indirectly, which significantly exceeds the horrors of twentieth-century wars and concentration camps.

ARNAUT: That was almost a fifth of the world's population,

nearly a billion people in today's numbers. No animal in nature causes so much harm to its own species the way humans do to their own. Humans find it difficult to change their nature. Today, in the twenty-first century, there are preconditions for humans to cast off what holds them back and look from a fresh perspective at the possibilities the world and society offer.

For example, Florence was a city-state, yet it was never an imperial power in the classical sense. Such conditions make it possible to imagine Machiavelli and find a justification for his understanding of politics. But the imperial ideas of Alexander the Great and the Romans were motivated not only by interests but, even more, and especially in the case of Alexander Great, by the ideal, a sense of honor, and principles that were sincerely believed to be the best, and that they should be imposed for that reason (with vanity, tremendous self-centeredness and need to perpetuate one's fame). That is in line with the considerations of the imperial idea of the great Russian thinker Berdyaev.

- The contemporary world is somehow confused and based on huge bureaucratic machinery. Besides the enormous apparatus and power, it lacks ideas and genuine rulers.

ARNAUT: There are great mechanisms of power that often mechanically apply the old principles without the original impulse. The machine operates based on numerous agreements, opinions, and changes of principles, as required. A selection is made between the principles of real politics or the principles of the struggle for democracy as instruments of political implementation, or rather for justification of the real interests hidden behind the struggle for democracy or anything else. At the same time, it is easy to forget that the rulers from the time of the ancient Greeks and Romans believed in their ideas and considered them the best. The modern world is motivated, no less (or maybe more), by greed, not by ideals. Therein lies one of the biggest problems.

- What is your opinion of the modern rulers from the historical perspective?

ARNAUT: The modern rulers are often megalomaniacs or psychopaths (which does not imply that many past ones were not the same) – fortunately, to a much lesser degree – or they are, predominantly, clowns, apparatchiks or ambitious ignoramuses who obtained knowledge through schooling, but know nothing of the world and society. That makes them even more dangerous because some possess extensive knowledge; they believe they are genuine rulers capable of addressing important issues. The truth is, however, that they lack a cultural base and upgrade for original and correct thinking, which is the basis for making the right decisions. They have the illusion of power, which is only formal. The opinion-churning machine makes decisions, while the rulers believe they are the ones who choose and make personal decisions. However, even when they choose, those are merely opinions skillfully served by the machine.

- Moral authorities like Solon or Pericles do not run the machine, and intellectual authorities like Aristotle do not influence it.

ARNAUT: The machine is run by countless „experts" possessing specialized knowledge. Although there is talk of global tendencies, no one can precisely sense what that is and how it should be implemented correctly. That is a matter of intellectual laziness and lack of courage. That laziness is fatal because it turns out it is easier to spend hundreds of billions of dollars, even trillions, on unnecessary work and wars than to invest some effort and nurture spirits possessing the gift of foresight and genuine ability to rule.

- But global tendencies have almost made your language extinct.

ARNAUT: That is correct. However, Europe was torn apart to

such a degree and ravaged by constant conflicts and contradictions. After all, all Romance languages originate from a single one – Latin, and that primary language is now dead. The whole of history is based on paradoxes. Languages are important, but are we fully aware of these paradoxes? If one language was the base for the Romance languages, while other Indo-European languages were the basis for, say, Slavic and Germanic languages, which developed from the same roots, then the historical process led to the distancing from those same genetic and linguistic roots, and not to their preservation. That means we do not have a complete and accurate picture of anything.

- That implies that belonging to larger groups is not bad, nor does it lead to identity violation but, among other things, to the return to broader identities that have already existed in history. If Hitler had been aware of the common genetic and linguistic roots of the Slavs and the Germans, he would have certainly toned down his madness to some extent.

ARNAUT: If the influential people in Hitler's time (or before the First World War and even earlier) had been more aware of the historical context, Hitler's rise would not have been possible.

- In your opinion, unification and the spirit of belonging to larger communities, as well as the identification with ideas that represent such a spirit, can be the answer to potential problems and a basis for further and more fruitful development. What is your vision of the Western world? What is the West?

ARNAUT: There is one big Europe and one big Western world; it spreads on all continents. Through Russia, Europe penetrates deep into Asia.

COUNTRIES AND IDEAS

From Moscow to Berlin and Washington
From Rome to Buenos Aires
From Lisbon to Rio de Janeiro
From Madrid to Mexico
From Paris to Montreal
From London to Sydney and Toronto
From Amsterdam to New York
One World, tradition, idea.

Every division is false. Family quarrels must not be a cause for madness.

- Is there one West and one Europe?

ARNAUT: There is one Europe. I believe all divisions of Europe into eastern, western, central, and southern parts are false and have no meaning or historical justification except for, perhaps, a geographical one. Russia is as much a part of the West as France or Germany. Eurasia is geographically one continent, and Russia occupies half of Europe and a large portion of Asia. America is the West, and so is Australia; for the last five centuries, Latin America has been part of the Western sphere. In my opinion, that is the Western world. This is one natural bloc. This whole bloc not only united Europe but also made the Western world. China has always been a world for itself, and the West has never had big problems with China. India is a world for itself, too. However, the Western world comes from the same Indo-European root. Apart from this, the bloc consists of parts of Asia and Africa, with the predominant influence of Islam.

That does not mean that the world should be monolithic. On the contrary, this should only serve as the basis for global and individual progress, similar to the *Risorgimento* in Italy. That does not imply the suppression of national cultures and languages unless the cultures themselves allow it through their negligence. A world like this, based on the principles of harmony and high ethical standards, can enable the flourishing of smaller cultures. At the same time, this does not mean erasing the borders either in Europe or between North and South America (or between the United States and Mexico). This applies instead to ideological unity and cooperation.

As I see it, this is the only way for the human race to avoid catastrophes or even self-destruction that potentially awaits it.

- Does that mean that the phenomenon of globalization is frequently misunderstood or rather misapplied? In other words, does it serve interests not in genuine globalization but in securing special interests in a globalized world?

ARNAUT: There is a vulgar concept of globalization, and globalization is in progress, regardless of the nomenclature of political and economic power. Self-proclaimed political and economic elites carry out vulgar globalization. That is where the biggest problem occurs, which stems from the fact that those who possess the greatest power, either political or economic, think that, at the same time, they possess the best opinion, too, which is often not the case. Namely, only the best opinion can be an elite one. An opinion that is not the best cannot be elite only because it is supported or created within the nomenclature of political and economic power.

Often, vulgar nationalism can serve as a recipe for climbing the ladder of political power, just as greed can be a recipe for economic rise. The problem with both is that both ascents' consequences are obscure. Both ascents lead toward an illusion because they create an atmosphere of false progress and false power. Everyone who sincerely fights for genuine progress fights for something long-lasting and predictable to the highest degree. Progress based on vulgar principles or a vulgar implementation of sublime tenets that serve as a mere form for something else is not genuine progress and, in its nature, is short-lived because it neglects the power of true value.

In that sense, the true elites are not those with formal political and economic power but those with the best opinions and vision. If the power elites stifle the real elites too much, the price is paid not only by the true elites but even more by the self-proclaimed elites who work to their detriment and, although unconsciously, slide toward self-destruction. The true elite's power does not rest on literal power but on the power of reason, values, and ethics. The power of the quasi-elites rests on arrogance, special interests, illusions, propaganda, seduction ... Behind the self-proclaimed elites of the political and economic powers, plutocracy, oligarchy, theocracy, or kleptocracy are often hidden (a new term used by American economist Michael Hudson). In the tendencies of such elites, there is nothing noble. Vulgar power is, in its nature, anti-cultural. Among other things, it cannot be elite according to ethical or aesthetic criteria.

- Is such a model of the world achievable under the natural criteria that are simultaneously rational and useful for the West, and how great is religion's role in this?

ARNAUT: This can only be achieved if one deviates in practice from the model, programs, and drafts of those who fight for it with insincere intentions. All such proponents of globalization (some of which are pretty famous) fight, on the one hand, for the so-called "open society" and, on the other, for a "global sheriff" (an expression coined by Soros). How honest can one be when fighting for an open society, which implies a greater degree of democracy and freedom, and, simultaneously, for the global sheriff, indicating some supreme controller or a covert, masked dictator? Such tendencies could potentially lead to horrendous consequences. Globalization may have a huge and positive role only if implemented following the interest of the whole that serves the interests of all its parts and only for universal empowerment, not only for the concentration of political and economic (financial) power in the hands of a handful of individuals. These tendencies may be the hidden agenda of many of those who fight for such programs, which could turn the rest of the world, including entire nations, into modern-day slavery in a different form.

Based on the natural criteria, it would be logical for Europe and Russia to gravitate toward each other. This does not mean Russia must be a member of the European Union (perhaps time should judge what is the best option). Still, some economic and military alliances should be formed, and time will show the best ways the European Community member countries should operate.

Following the collapse of communism in Russia, it has become clear to everyone that Russia will not, nor does it want to, attack Germany, the Czech Republic, or Poland. It's natural that Europe, as one continent, should cooperate fully and be in sync with Russia, which occupies half of the European continent. This would be a natural and logical development of events because who can defend Europe better than Europe itself, in economic and military terms? The Cold War has long been over, so there is no need for artificial antagonism between Russia and the rest of Europe. Russia is not Europe's enemy, and there is no reason for the rest of Europe to be the enemy of Russia. This kind of Europe may best consolidate the Western world in cooperation with America.

- How big a role can religion play in this?

ARNAUT: Faith can be one of the essential cohesive elements. However, if the world is moving towards unification, faith should also be one naturally. Its primary center can be in Rome, while other centers with religious leaders, who would be *primus inter pares*, would exist in other western cities, as was the case before the splitting of the church. In this case, the sole difference would be a greater number of centers set up on the American and Australian continents as well: one faith, one Western world.

There is already a vast infrastructure, and without major disturbances within the structure over a certain period, a single faith may be established, one closer to God and humans. All previous religions have alienated humans from God and God from humans.

Religions appropriate the right to hold a belief and faith, which is the individual's inalienable right, regardless of religion. The faithful need God, not a mere nominal religion. Nominal religions are fit for governance, not for faith. God cannot be acquired, nor can faith. Faith is a natural feeling that arises and develops in one's direct relationship with the world.

In previous religions, books were instruction manuals for interpreting God and connecting with him. Therefore, they tend to convince us that if God's course is completed and the instructions are mastered, the knowledge of God can be readily obtained, and the path to paradise is guaranteed. That is both impossible and unnatural. No book written by the human hand is a ticket to paradise, nor can it be a sufficient and final source of knowledge about God. The only true divine book is the world, and a greater understanding of the world leads to a greater understanding of God. The only path to God is the path through the World. The only book containing all the answers is the World. To interpret God is to interpret the World. The World is the only Bible.

- Please continue with the sestinas.

LOVE AND HATE

Love can only be selfishly selfless;
Mad hatred is loneliness desolate.
As from other people's faces love shines,
Appropriating the world with its smiles,
Hatred's pure love radiates from the prey
With a distinct taste of blood in its mouth.

It deceives and lures with its toxic mouth –
Hatred is deeply selfish selflessly,
Its life is impossible without prey,
That's why it's always alone, desolate,
Its face resplendent with disastrous smiles,
From within the heart, it can never shine.

It is not the heart but love that now shines;
It keeps the food for the world in its mouth,
While looking for happiness in all smiles,
Revitalized by strength, fully selfless.
Thus are revived all places desolate
From the very root of love's helpless prey.

Always well-fed, in constant lack of prey,
Even in the yawning darkness, love shines
Feeding light to all places desolate,
It never seeks joy in hideous mouths,
As its pure magic, already selfless
Saturates the darkness with its bright smiles.

Hatred constantly seeks prey in the smiles,
Its light is impossible without prey,
The bleakness of its evil is selfless,

From deep within it, dawn can never shine,
It dwells concealed inside the somber mouth,
Where no Sun warms the places desolate.

The desert is not always desolate –
Light caresses it with its tender smiles,
And hate dries it with its ravenous mouth –
It devours it in lack of other prey;
And even in the desert, love still shines
And blooms all around, completely selfless.

Without prey, hatred dies all desolate
While love remains to shine from all the smiles –
It is selfless food to all needy mouths.

THE SECRET

Is life merely an awakened secret
That emerges straight from inside its sleep
Or is life perchance a secret that dreams?
The secret weaves tall tales and life itself;
The secret of life births the fairy tale;
Life's a superb secret and deception.

The secret of life lies in deception,
Life is entrusted with only one secret;
Without deception, there's no happy tale,
Life confides in the true secret of sleep.
I can't tell if I'm deception itself
Or life, or a deceptive secret's dream.

Is it deception, does life only dream
Or is life toyed with by sheer deception,
That is a mystery to life itself;

Or deception brings joy to the secret
Awakening life from a rueful sleep
As it's occupied by the fairy tale.

Deception shines from omnipotent fairy tale
And instructs life in the science of dreams;
Without dreams, there is no happy sleep;
A tale is the truth, not a deception,
Its heart is the dwelling of the secret,
A tale is joyfulness and life itself.

Without tales, darkness engulfs life itself.
In life, life is dreamed up by fairy tales.
Every tale holds the murmurs of secret,
Only in fairy tales, one can still dream:
In them, there's still life's playful deception,
Every life emerges straight from the sleep

And thus it awakens itself from sleep,
As secret's deception and life itself,
Deceived by itself, not by deception.
The world is nothing but a fairy tale,
So that life would start to glimmer and dream,
Just a luminously outlined secret.

Deception is life awakened from sleep,
To dream in the light, while darkness itself
Is neither a fairy tale nor secret.

CHIMERA

Is the world a chimera or the truth,
Or is the world's truth a mere chimera?
Nothing's more dazzling than the open sea
Awaking from the sea of illusions,
Nothing's more dazzling than serenity –
It is the food of dreams and elation.

There's no world without divine elation –
The dream of the world is its only truth,
The world's wings spread out in serenity.
Winged reality is no chimera,
It guards the world against dark's illusions
And waves to it out in the open sea,

Overcomes the dark from the open sea.
Armed with the power of its elation,
The world grows from the sea of illusions,
The world is God's power and His one truth;
To light the world of dreams and chimeras
From its heart, it issues serenity.

Illusion enables serenity
Smiling at the world from the open sea;
The root of the world sprouts from chimeras;
Without them, there's no dream or elation.
The world's here, and everything; it's the truth
That through fire births the life of illusion.

It wards off illusion with illusion,
To illuminate its serenity.
It thinks to itself: I am the one truth,

Through the world's eye, out in the open sea
It sees its fires, power of elation,
All luminous forms and all chimeras.

All distances blaze from the chimeras,
The world's more real than its illusion,
Without dreams, he can feel no elation;
He proudly rises from serenity
To conquer and claim all dark open seas,
For the world is the divine dream and truth.

In serenity shines a chimera:
At sea, there's a watchful eye of illusion.
The truth of the world blooms in elation.

SECRET AND CHIMERA
(REALITY)

The night hides the secret of chimeras
That appear in daytime as a mirage;
More enigmatic than any secret,
More visible than its reality;
Life itself is their one and only child
That keeps their memory in dream-like tales.

The child retells the dream in life-like tales,
It elevates life above chimeras,
The magic in the world begets a child,
Whereas the Child-World is not a mirage.
The light shines from the heart of reality,
Finding strength in the heart of the secret;

Distance is the charm and strength of the secret
That to all shapes and forms narrates its tales
Of fire and luminous reality;
From the secret, there shine the chimeras;
Only reality's not a mirage,
Because it feeds fire to its only child.

The universe's secret is its child
That shines from the dark core of the secret.
The world can never be a mere mirage –
The secret shares its secret in its tales;
The secret does shine, not the chimera –
Light sings from within its reality.

Ray language's spoken by reality
Through rays gives birth to the secret's child

To repel advances of chimeras
Offering answers stemming from secrets,
It tells of itself in its ray-like tales –
The truth itself appears like a mirage.

The ray shines even when it's a mirage;
That's a great fortune of reality –
Immortality secured by the tales,
As the splendid song of the merry child
Proclaims the sacred kiss of the secret.
What shines is the child, not the chimera,

Chimera turns tales into a mirage,
Awakes things from secret reality –
The child shares the secret in ray-like tales.

SURFACE

The depth shines from the surfaces,
Each surface only depths may show,
A ray of the dark comes from whiteness;
The light of darkness overflows,
Telling tales of deep distances,
Through the world, the depth with light rows.

The universe in its light rows,
Lures with sparks from the surfaces,
Spreading dreams from dark distances.
On the surface itself, it will show;
Into songs, the light overflows,
The surfaces sing from whiteness,

In constellations of whiteness:
So that through darkness he could row
His beauty starts to overflow
By new rays from the surfaces,
By virtue of rays, beauty shows.
Hurled by rays from a vast distance

He shines from deepest distances;
All the stars make up his whiteness:
It's darkness in light his face shows.
In His own light, God dreams and rows,
Smiling at the world from surfaces,
In bright smiles, his dreams overflow.

As its tale in rays overflows,
The dark sea grows from the distance,
Through the rays light from surfaces

Spreads out creating whiteness,
Darkness flies through the light and rows
That God's secret meaning does show,

Through his light every depth will show
Big bright birds that space overflow.
The world in its own light does row
Glowing gaily from distances.
Every depth becomes its whiteness
And sings from gleaming surfaces.

Surface into light overflows.
Birthing God has shown by whiteness,
The distance in its rays does row.

DEPTH

Depth is the greatest mystery
That God in his heart may conceal;
God shines from dark profundities
And secrets into shapes reveals;
Light is his greatest sorcery
That the world into the depths spills.

All over the world, the light spills
Atoms as signs of mystery,
Devilish sparks and sorcery,
And of the dark rays, which conceal
The depth that bright letters reveal
In the language of profundity

In deep sparkling profundity
Of sparks that into the world spill
So dark worlds in light will reveal
Through thoughts, to revive mystery,
Its creator a fire conceals.
Light is a divine sorcery.

A world rousing from sorcery
With his allure's profundity
In the darkness, a spark conceals.
Into the world, Blazing God spills
Through stars, as does light mystery;
In bright mystery, God's revealed

Into notes, all his light's revealed.
The world guards light against sorcery,
His World is his grand mystery –

He dazzles from profundity –
Into the world, through light, it's spilled.
In his heart, his secret's concealed.

His face, the conductor conceals,
Each star's in harmony revealed;
Meanwhile, into the day rays spill
From the light of dark sorcery,
Through the music of profundity,
The sacred, divine mystery.

Divine mystery is revealed,
Conceals the face of profundity;
Sorcery in the world is spilled.

- We don't know precisely the truth, illusion, or sorcery, yet we feel the world around us. What is the truth?

ARNAUT: Nobody knows what it is. I would say that the World is the truth, and I believe in the World.

- Can words express the truth?

ARNAUT: What are words for?

- These are the terms and ways we explain the world names we give to phenomena, ideas, and objects.

ARNAUT: What if we give phenomena false names or names that do not represent what they should represent?

- Then the situation becomes complicated. Then, we think and argue about something we either do not know anything about or believe that we know, although that is not what we think it is.

Therefore, we use the terms; we try to express different phenomena with the same words.

ARNAUT: What is religion?

- A word.

ARNAUT: What does this word represent?

- Faith.

ARNAUT: In what?

- In God.

ARNAUT: Who creates religions?

- People who claim to speak in the name of God.

ARNAUT: What is God?

- The word that indicates the origin of the World. It must be the truth that you claim nobody knows what it is. But you claim that the World is God.

ARNAUT: People achieve all this with words. God is not a word. Or, if he is, then it is a different thing. It is not a word that people can express in letters. The words that God uses are different from human ones. He writes his book with galaxies and atoms. No book can explain God, or the Truth, or the World. All the world's matter, with all its particles, would not be enough to write such a book. It is impossible. The World is the truth, and God's Bible.

- People claim to write God's words, not theirs.

ARNAUT: So, we have to take their word for it?

- We must.

ARNAUT: And their claims are words, too?

- Yes.

ARNAUT: Does that mean we have to believe in the word of their claims that their words are not their words?

- It looks that way.

ARNAUT: All we have is their word?

- Yes. What are the right words? Does God need our words? What is God's word?

ARNAUT: The World.

- It sounds effortless. It can fit into a single word. Why do many people write and produce so many words when they can often do all that with a few words?

ARNAUT: People intentionally create the wind in their words or because they do not know better.

- Then there are no limits because the wind is impossible to create. It's impossible to turn it into a word. It's like alchemy. The wind that people make seems only like some abstract language breeze. And this never becomes a wind, so we need new and new words, fresh and new words, to get to the wind source. The World is no longer the World; it is a word; the World becomes an interpretation. And if God is the World, it turns out, in words, that

God is neither God nor the World but a word. As language cannot produce enough words on the way to God or the origin of the World, the word is lost in the windy city of words, in which words are the only wind, yet there is no real wind.

ARNAUT: It seems so.

- This means that there is a lot of wind between these words.

ARNAUT: No, not between them, but in them.

- Is it possible to drive the wind out of them?

ARNAUT: It is not necessary to force the wind out of words. It is essential to eliminate the words with the wind in them.

- It seems that most words are like that; if we eliminate all, there would be few left.

ARNAUT: Those that remain come to life, and the wind doesn't suffocate them. How can they be heard when verbal typhoons and hurricanes blow from all sides?

- This means that five hundred pages can fit into five.

ARNAUT: Yes. And much more.

- How?

ARNAUT: I am thinking of five hundred pages worth five million, which you can reduce to five. That means five pages may have a value of five million.

- Do the banished words have any odds of redemption?

ARNAUT: Of course. I'm not saying that we should kill any word. I claim that words or terms should mean what they are to represent. If words say one thing and express another, then these are neither words nor terms. It's magic, which is tantamount to a lie. But all words that are purified and become terms and mean what they say can return. If this happens, you will realize that many of them, when revealed, have many other, more essential meanings, such as artistic and literary, for example.

Art and literature primarily strive for the beauty, contact, and silent conversation they offer readers, spectators, or listeners. Fiction in art is wonderful, yet fantasy, sold as something else, not as fantastic literature, betrays its nature, significance, and readers.

- Is the conversation you refer to possible if some words are banished?

ARNAUT: Yes. Because we must not allow being held hostage to words with different meanings from those they express. Also, it is not our task to purify them; our mission is only to disclose them. When you stop being a hostage, it will be possible to talk about ideas.

- But words cannot do this alone. You're talking about them as humans. Words are just words. People give them meaning – correct or incorrect. Only people can do this part of work, not words.

ARNAUT: All people hiding behind these words hold us hostage. And why should we be their hostages? Once these people realize that we do not want and will no longer be their hostages, they will expose and disclose the true meaning of these words. Those aware shall recognize the truth, but those deluded or mistakenly believing shall come to their senses. These people are efficient and know what they are doing well. They will strive for dialogue once no one listens to and believes them.

- Dialogue is essential in everything

ARNAUT: As much as people think that disagreement, or a different view on things, is a source of trouble or misunderstanding, this is not the case. Only demagogic appearances, unwavering truth, ideology, and religion greatly exclude the possibility of a real conversation. On the other hand, if we are free from complexes and personal vanity, we understand that different opinions lead to a greater truth. If our aim is real, we should not be bothered by a different view; on the contrary, it should be desirable because it helps us strive for the same goal.

- It seems logical because if everyone thought the same or had the same knowledge, we would not need a conversation or dialogue. The same opinions are the death of conversation.

ARNAUT: Different opinions are the speech of the World. The World consists of many that are not and cannot be uniform. If everyone were the same or thought the same, then a lot in the world would not make sense – it would be a mechanical division of the same thing, or innumerable cloned, without meaning, objective, and purpose.

- Conversation implies different ideas, which do not automatically mean a different opinion but a different approach to issues. With the same concepts and ideas, we can access various matters, the same problems, or other concepts and ideas. If we add the predisposition of individuals to this, a multitude of ways is inevitable.

ARNAUT: Although there seem to be many ideas, they are mostly invalid. The truth is that there are countless ideas, yet what causes the biggest problem is not a large number of ideas but a small number of variously interpreted views. The problem arises with, so to speak, big ideas. Since these ideas are, in their essence, abstract, they cannot be covered by one opinion unless it is about a religion (which, again, is a sum of views). Thus, many ideas are born, and a conversation arises and becomes possible.

- The problem, then, is not in ideas but in opinions.

ARNAUT: The problem is not in ideas because without ideas, even inexplicable, a human being loses the driving force of thought. Different opinions, but only those honest, lead to a better understanding of ideas. If a view is imposed and harms the right ideas, it does not lead to dialogue and better performance but instead to demagoguery. If the opinion serves the ideas, it is useful even if you disagree.

Different opinions are like different rays or colors in a world where each part has its place and role. The World would be less rich if we had fewer colors, but this does not mean that every opinion has value, the right to survival, longevity, and color. Natural phenomena, including colors, have their place in the context of an almost perfect and immense organism. People's opinions must stand the test of time.

- There have always been huge differences among philosophers, artists, politicians, and rulers.

ARNAUT: As we all know, Tolstoy believed that Shakespeare's works were "bloody ravings" and considered Nietzsche "stupid and abnormal."

- Bertrand Russell thought that Nietzsche was not an academic philosopher and did not like the concept of the overman, whom he saw as ruthless and deprived of love.

ARNAUT: He resented Nietzsche's lack of understanding of Christian love, and Bertrand Russell had a whole book about it – *Why I am not a Christian*. Such views are important because they lead to crystallization.

As for the academic way of thinking, viewing, or philosophizing, one might ask who Socrates was. He was quite different from the modern concept of a philosopher and philosophy, especially from academic philosophers' ideas, even though the question is whether academies and academic philosophers would be what they are today without him. For, without Socrates, would there be Plato as a philosopher? The student of the 'non-academic' philosopher founded the first real academy, from which the lyceum would merge later and everything that gave the basis for developing the European education system.

- Socrates lived more as an artist than a scientist. He spent much time on the streets (sometimes from morning to night) watching people and talking to them.

ARNAUT: Socrates saw the whole World as an academy. He knew his relationship with others; direct experience helped him understand more than books did. He knew that a direct relationship with the World, or nature, offered him more than human, limited responses. Socrates knew all this was worthless without a method or the correct way of thinking, born and developed through self-discipline and a sincere attitude toward the World. Socrates knew that all of this was worth nothing without predisposition. Ultimately, Socrates knew it was possible to come to some conclusions about the world and humanity if all this fit.

It was challenging to outperform Socrates in the arguments, although it does not mean that Socrates did not sometimes wish that somebody could outdo him. For all we know about him, he searched for the truth, which means he would not just accept the opposite argument – if it were indisputable – he would have done it with great pleasure because it would help him to be less lonely in his intentions. It would help to crystallize further and improve the knowledge he had acquired himself.

- Unlike many other philosophers, Socrates did not create the wind in his words.

ARNAUT: He didn't. He sincerely interpreted the World, endowed with immense ingenuity and insight, which was the base of his curing, killing argument, and understanding of the World and phenomena.

A philosopher strives for a deep understanding of the World. All those who contribute to this understanding with their interpretations and visions are philosophers. Therefore, Einstein claimed he had learned more about Euclidean geometry from Dostoyevsky than most scientists. In the supreme creation, creators from various fields touch and become, in some way, philosophers.

If a musician, even instinctively, would not understand the philosophy of music, then there would be no Beethoven, Mozart, Albinoni, or Puccini, not to mention all of them. If a poet (writer) did not understand, at least intuitively, the philosophy of poetry, prose, drama (the arts), then there would be no Homer, Sophocles (and the other two tragedians), Dante, Shakespeare, or Cervantes. Without the philosophy of science, although intuitively understood, there would be no Archimedes, Ptolemy, Heron, Newton, Galileo, Kepler, or Tesla. Philosophy is in everything and is the basis of everything. Each superb poet is partly a philosopher, every scientist, every musician, every top-level doctor, or an engineer. A philosopher in a chemist finds a new drug; a philosopher reveals a human application of light in Edison or Tesla. Neither Tesla nor Edison invented light or electricity (current); these are natural phenomena that exist independently of them, but the philosopher in a scientist knows that natural wonders can be decrypted and, most importantly, placed into the service of humanity.

A human being, conditionally speaking, cannot create anything new but can penetrate deeper into the World. Human innovation is about other people, not about the world. Even if they were novelties globally, their possibility was already in the World's old content. The World cannot be surprised by anything, not through any wonders. If humans lived outside the World, they could add something to the World. Since humans are the World's product, they cannot add or subtract anything from the World. They can only beautify, enrich, and improve it.

A perfect world is a world without exit, without the ability to move. Motion generates meaning. In the World, everything is given and cannot be significantly changed. We can only change ourselves and strive for an even greater understanding of the World. Through discoveries, the World renews itself and rejoices. Penetrating its depths is an award and appreciation of the World, confirmation that its size and value make sense.

Everything that humans create is human novelties that are born on the way of the World. The form of the World is the way of each of its creatures. Each new story is the story of the ancient World, which develops and tries to establish and measure its strength and meaning. There is a variety of a living World – it allows you to talk. With their novelties or scientific and artistic works, human beings mimic the World using their tools and language; they bring meaning into the void and contribute to the creation of the World by finding good reasons. Beautification and ascent oppose the monotony and lethargy.

Beauty encourages movement. Realization and experience of beauty are a source of pleasure and reason enough to move. The point is not the question of meaning. The point is a matter of life and death. Denying the purpose is equal to denying the World. To deny the World is to deny life. The World itself is the point; its very existence. If the World does not make sense, then life does not make sense because the World is life. If this is the case, then there is just nothing. And nothing has neither meaning nor nonsense. What is better – the World, with the sense and nonsense, or Nothingness without nonsense, but also without purpose? It's all about motion, construction, and beauty. And man's presence has a reason and purpose if there is a world without reason.

- That's why you harvest the wind rather than create it.

ARNAUT: Yes.

- It is impossible to create the wind. To harvest wind is impossible, too.

ARNAUT: It is possible to harvest something from the world, and what we harvest seems definite and simple. One word hides the other; one wind hides all the winds, all the worlds, and words. The World is one. It is not necessary to divide it by innumerable superfluous words.

- Words can't divide it.

ARNAUT: Words cannot divide the World, but they can distance us from the World with their cunning power.

- Then the World moves away from us in words.

ARNAUT: Just like raging winds that bend us and bear left-right, throw up-down, raise, and again throw down.

- This means that a word separates us from the World.
ARNAUT: What separates us from the World is not a word but a fake word and an excess of words.

-Wouldn't it be more comfortable to talk less?

ARNAUT: Yes, but then the words that do not mean anything are discovered.

- This is a maze of words. However, the matter is more straightforward than it seems at first glance. Why do people go through so much trouble when it appears they can somehow solve the issue?

ARNAUT: The goal of many is not to say something but to take something from the World that does not belong to them.

- It's magic.

ARNAUT: Power is much more important to wind or word producers than words *per se*. They do not live by the word but instead off words.

- It looks like a devil's pact.

ARNAUT: What is the Devil?

- Word.

ARNAUT: Whose word?

- People use it.

ARNAUT: To express what?

- Darkness and evil.

ARNAUT: Again, do we need to take their word for it?

- People have said that the Devil is the opposite of God – Satan, who rebels against God, the supreme angel.

ARNAUT: What is Lucifer, or who is it?

- Someone who steals the light from the darkness and brings it into the night.

ARNAUT: It's a little strange. He steals the light from the darkness and brings it out of the night to shine on the World. How can he represent evil and darkness if he opposes the darkness and would have to be a representation of evil? Or, perhaps it is better to say: how can the word representing him be all that it means if he is someone who carries the light?

Often, the goal of words is not to represent what they claim to represent but to produce confusion or winds. Lucifer was the Morning Star, representing the planet Venus. Can the Morning Star, or the Light Bringer (Light-Bearer), be what it purports to be when the word means someone who brings the light? These meanings, which people subsequently added, have nothing to do with Lucifer.

- You say that God is the World, and the World's life energy is a kind of fire or light. Does this mean that Lucifer is the World?

ARNAUT: What else can he be? There is nothing outside the World other than emptiness. A world without light is a sleeping God. In such a world, he is without the void within. Since there are no gaps in him, he disappears, in himself, swallowed by his greatness. Almost infinite size reduces him to zero. It is an undivided God. It is God without the World, the God without movement. Without emptiness, he is nothing. When he releases himself into the void and darkness, he wakes up. He realizes this by absorbing the vacuum into himself and by dividing himself.

That's how the World is born: the light, a multitude from One that embarks on a journey.

It is a rebellion of God against himself, who saves himself from himself with multitudes. Multitude enables the way. It is the only possible duality – one and the many (oneness and multitude). Oneness is the World or the God who sleeps; many (multitude) is the awakened God or Lucifer. The multitude represents the means and modalities of the World's poles, among which is evil, the source of which people mistakenly identify with the Devil or Satan, a rogue angel. And the renegade angel is none other than the God who comes to freedom from his bondage. God is dying because of his size, fulfillment, and infallibility. Salvation is in the division through the conquest of emptiness or Nothingness.

- If the World is light, this means that Lucifer, or the World, is the only son of God, divided into many parts to find a sense of the way through nowhere. Someone who brings the light, or who is the light, cannot be evil and cannot constitute the gloom.

ARNAUT: The word most distant from the true meaning is darkness. Everyone equates darkness with the dark forces, evil, and the strange, as if the whole evil World is hiding in the dark. And in fact, darkness is the most innocent thing. Darkness is not a thing; darkness is nothing – a real emptiness and darkness without a world in itself. You cannot imagine anything cleaner than emptiness.

- How can such emptiness, or darkness, represent the evil or the Devil? Nothing is just nothing. There is no evil or good in it, neither love nor hate nor movement. Nothing is sinless.
ARNAUT: Nothing is sinless. You imagine Paradise as a place where there is no sin. It means Paradise is nothing. Only the World can dirty the Nothing, bringing movement and possibility of good and evil. If we imagine God as something completely sinless, it

can only be – nothing since only nothing would be a fair and accurate description of it.

- Does it mean that God is nothing?

ARNAUT: Buddhists think so, but it is God's primordial state. God lives through the World. His only option for life is the World. And the World is not nothing.

- God is the only rebel who rebels against the darkness and emptiness. He does not accept the purity of the immobile World and stainless gaps. He wins by dividing and polarizing himself.

ARNAUT: All that any word means is a story about him and represents him. There is nothing outside of him. Darkness without God is absolute emptiness. Nothing can rebel against God. There is no way out of him. He seizes the void and anything that rebels, rebels in his framework, traveling through him. He is the supreme rebel.

- That means he is the Devil?

ARNAUT: He is all that is conceivable and inconceivable, including every imaginable and unimaginable thing. Devil is just a word. This word represents the rebel and someone who brings discomfort. The restlessness of what? Nobody can introduce turmoil to the World because the World, or God, is what it is. The World is restless; the World brings unrest into the void and darkness. Thus, the World or God becomes a sinner who disturbs the heavenly peace of Nothingness or emptiness. This concept of God you interpret as the Devil. Both are the words. All words represent the World. Outside the World, there is nothing but emptiness; the void is immaculate and non-existent, meaning it can hide no Devil.

- Does it mean the World is a rebellious God who chooses life instead of purity, heaven, and Nothingness?

ARNAUT: Yes. And that's the price of fall. It is, in fact, an ascent into life, not a fall, but it also implies a mistake, pain, and everything that makes life what it is. God accepts the price. It is another matter that those who cannot take the World's polarization reject the possibility of error, a somewhat inevitable deviation that confirms the law or evil in God, and generate ideas about opposing forces, which is impossible. God is not a country or city from which one can escape or steal anything; no one can act beyond it. Nothing comes out of God, and nothing can enter him except the emptiness. Since there is no way out of God, it is impossible to revolt against him. Rebellion means duality, the possibility of separation, where the other end opposes God. But this is impossible because outside, there is nothing, not even the evil itself.

Evil would not upset us if it were something in the void of darkness. It would be something foreign and unknown. It disturbs us because it is not in the dark but is often visible and recognizable. After all, it is among us, in us. It inhabits the World and us. Our anger at the Devil is anger at ourselves because we do not want to admit that it's us or the World, God's World, so everything we do not wish or we do not want to face is attributed to forces beyond us. The beauty of the World and the evil come from the World and not outside the World. The only sinless Paradise is the World outside the World. But this is nothing or death.

Life, in its vastness and hierarchy, means all this. If humans want a world without evil or a world without sin, they must drive the Devil out of themselves. Forcing him out of the World with words does not mean anything because he continues to live in us independently of the words or pointing to the abstract force outside of us that does not exist.

- If we banish him out of ourselves, then we will not have to talk about him.

ARNAUT: When you crush the Devil in you, he will disappear along with his rebellion.

- Is Lucifer a rebellious son, the revolutionary World, or a rebellious God?

ARNAUT: Lucifer is a son; God is a father and son. God needed the rebel son to bear the World out of himself in a loving embrace with the darkness and emptiness.

- Words seem to introduce beauty and value to the world, but they also introduce chaos.

ARNAUT: God and Lucifer are just words that people invented. That is why I use them not to develop anything new and create even more confusion. One word can mean one thing and represent another; the other could mean another and represent the first. That is the problem of language. That is the power of those who converted the deception into their strength. They manage to hunt and enslave souls without resistance, without a weapon. They produce linguistic winds.

- It seems like we do not know anything about anything. We talk about something and imagine something else. It turns out that this word is nothing. It leads us to no God or knowledge. It is a prank and not a word.
ARNAUT: Yes.

- So we cannot trust their word.

ARNAUT: No.

- People are unreliable.

ARNAUT: The words are unreliable.

- But people make words. It means that people are unreliable, as well as words.

ARNAUT: Yes, but if we understand that words are unreliable, people will lose their power. Words live, although people are dead. They do not affect us; their words do.

- Words imprison us. Words seem more important than we think and can achieve more than weapons. When you fight someone, you always have a chance. Maybe someday you'll gain better weapons or somehow prevail, or the enemy will get tired. But the word is tireless. As long as you believe in it, it lives. Then the opponent can rule over you even when you are unaware of it because you believe his word and think he is your friend. You think he offers answers and salvation.

ARNAUT: So it seems.

- Arnaut! Arnaut! It's pretty disappointing. It means that the greatest enemies may be those that we consider friends.

ARNAUT: Yes.

- Very sad.
ARNAUT: Very.

- Is there a possibility of knowledge?

ARNAUT: I cannot say anything about that except to suggest something that might satisfy your desire.

- And what is that?

ARNAUT: There is a river, which is not like other rivers but is also water and light. I sometimes swim in it, especially when something is unclear to me. Thus swimming opposite the light of this river, I often get a response to what I'm expecting.

- It's not dangerous?

ARNAUT: Not if you're honest. Nobody can trick this river, and I would not suggest anyone who is not completely honest jump into it.

- All right.

ARNAUT: Almost no one knows about this river. It hides in the woods, not far from here. We'll get there quickly.

- Well, we're already here. Will I learn to make sestinas and sing about knowledge in sestinas while swimming?

ARNAUT: If you are sincere, you will. That's how I learned. The river's light leads to another dimension and opens the door to knowledge. Jump now without thinking and fear, and scream, sing, pray. Do whatever it takes to get the information and secret knowledge.

- So I jumped into the river.

THE POSSIBILITY OF COGNITION

I

Is there a possibility of cognition?
Here in the light, I examine the Creator:
What is the truth, and what is just deceptiveness?
Is deception the truth of your comprehension
That ever takes me straight to the doorstep of yours,
Whereas in my dream, I pray for the emergence
Of a random spark of knowledge from the darkness
That lies dormant deep inside all creation
So that from its core, it may issue forth all bright
And lift the universe through its elevation,
In the light to experience the resurgence
And so the divine truth could start casting its light?

So that the truth conspicuously casts its light,
And that there will burst the light of my cognition
So that it will light up and shine in my eyes bright,
And my light will mark the start of your resurgence,
So that the light will sing from your comprehension.
The light ray that is awakened from the darkness
Is truth more brilliant than the Creator;
It soars on rays from the core of all creation,
Which is the resting place of all deceptiveness,
Warmed by the very light of your elevation,
So that the light could announce a new emergence,
The truth that will shine from the heart of yours.

That rose blossoms and sprouts out of the heart of yours,
That rose of veracity that casts its true light
When in the eye, a spark of knowledge emerges
So that light can unravel its comprehension,

To whisper the truth from deep within its darkness,
And to lead to the very source of cognition
At the secret reception with the Creator.
It is integrity; it is not deceptiveness;
The truth at the apex of its elevation
That appears before the eyes radiant and bright,
Paving the way for the secret's resurgence,
To the light that hovers above all creation.

O secret spark from the midst of all creation,
Reveal yourself and translate the true meaning of yours,
So that your word may start to shine out of darkness,
That it may shine in the waking world's emergence,
And there may sprout the spark of your comprehension
When in the brain, your word will start casting its light
And recall the exalting joint elevation
On the enlightened journeys of the Creator.
A face is hidden from yours by deceptiveness
With the divine light's immediate resurgence.
That is the truth of veritable cognition –
It rises from the darkness to appear all bright.

It is your Sun that shines out of the darkness bright,
Rising from the very bottom of creation;
In the vastness of the dark sea, it emerges
To give birth to the chance of your elevation,
And new possibilities for your cognition
Awakened in the glory of the Creator.
The Wise Star that glimmers from the depths of darkness
Leads one on a lasting journey to comprehension.
Sometimes, even the truth can be deceptiveness
Which on a lasting journey starts casting its light;
It protects itself from the intellect of yours,
'Til the revelation of the truth's resurgence.

Announce your secret truth's imminent resurgence
So that the world in your truth may radiate bright,
And so that, when in my dream the light emerges,
I would remember your divine elevation
As I flew toward the heart of comprehension,
Looking throughout the dark sea for the Creator,
As I fought to repel advancements of darkness
While being on the path to final cognition,
I prayed to darkness in the dream to cast its light
With rays that radiate outside all creation
And aid me to soar up toward the court of yours
A place where there is no room for deceptiveness.

There's no possibility of deceptiveness
When the light of the world finally resurges
And when the power of your thought from the darkness
Rises from the bowels of all creation
And when my eyes engulfed in the proper light
Of the enchantment of ecstatic cognition,
Razing obstacles en route to the Creator
Bathed in the flaming light of elevation,
And in the fragrances of the body of yours
Your beauty in its entirety emerges
And from my heart, there issues forth the newly bright
Clandestine wisdom of ancient comprehension.

Nourished by the splendor of your comprehension
The truth sprouts as the flower of deceptiveness,
So that in the darkness, it could appear all bright,
In its strongest light to announce the emergence
Of the whisper of your heart on my path of yore
To soar up on the wings of my elevation
On the journey to the only true cognition
As it shines its light to warm me from the darkness,

And inside my heart, to begin to cast its light
And in my spirit to announce its resurgence
As I follow God to the end of creation.
My truth does blossom from within the Creator,

And my fragrance feeds me inside the Creator,
My flower does subsist on your comprehension,
My light radiates from within the heart of yours,
My fortitude sprouts from my one (re)cognition
That you are the truth, that you're not deceptiveness,
That you are the one hope of divine creation
Awakened from the lifeless, infinite darkness
To glow with the brilliance of elevation,
To preserve its world and to persevere all bright,
So that the truth to all may announce resurgence,
And the secret's face cast its heavenly light
In dreams and beyond to impart its emergence.

With the light of sleep, there appears and emerges
The knowledge that awakens from the Creator
To appear above my shadowy path all bright.
Shielded from the darkness by bright deceptiveness
I seek my path through the chaos of creation
With each cautious step on the path of cognition.
The warm light of the goal beckons from the darkness,
The warmth engulfs me of the heart of yours
I remember the old stroll and your smiling light,
Inside the dream, I recall old comprehension
As I dream about a new one's close resurgence,
So that your heart in mine causes elevation.

When your heart in mine ignites elevation,
The truth undergoes momentary emergence;
It protects me as I recall your creation,

Replenish from the source of your comprehension,
And struggle while being lured by deceptiveness,
To find and follow the clandestine trail of yours.
Above the paths, your Sun appears and lingers bright,
Offers a glimpse of eternal cosmic light
In the eternal realm of the one Creator
That nourishes the tree of divine cognition.
Ray initiates the divine thought's resurgence
As the beasts menacingly skulk in the darkness.

Your island radiates softly from the darkness
And in the eyes, the spark appears to rouse the light
When your Sun from the sea's deepest depths emerges:
Only the lifeless darkness is deceptiveness,
While submerged in the sea, my keeps shining bright,
And my heart declares light's Sun imminent resurgence,
And light begins to grow out of the heart of yours,
And light begins to bloom from the heart of creation,
Rousing the light of supreme comprehension.
The island shines on from the heart of the Creator,
Rewarding the world with rays of elevation
While sailing toward the ultimate cognition.

The truth casts the light of divine elevation
With darkness to make bright the birth of creation;
It springs from the darkness, radiates from comprehension
Your deceptiveness – the light of dreams' resurgence.
Without the Creator, there's no true cognition,
Or the world of yours to declare its emergence.

II

Down the river, through the whirls, I swim and question –
Where is the resting place of the truth still untold?
And right before me, the light begins to appear;
As if in a dream, the truth under my inspection,
Before my eyes, stretches and begins to unfold,
To tell of the path in the truth and multiply
The way of the ray by which the path is revived
On its journey into the Outer Dominions.
The path offers a path and tells us who is he
That emerges from a memory of its own:
In the light, it attempts its true self to espy
And puts the world in the seat of authority.

Trail leads me to the light's seat of authority,
And inside my dream, I still put forth the question,
Is that the path or the truth, or does simply he,
Inside my dream, attempts his own self to espy;
Down the blazing trail, I put under inspection
The light itself as it is being self-revived.
I see that the light is the very truth untold;
In light is the root of the Outer Dominions;
From its dream, the Universe begins to appear
To scribble down the truth of the dream of his own;
With rays, it impregnates itself and multiplies,
Directing the bright game of the world to unfold.

In his dream, he plays the game that slowly unfolds,
By light ascends to the seat of authority,
By dividing the Universe, he multiplies.
Light awakens in my dream under my inspection,
With the rays and light of the Sun, he is revived;
I stroll ever further as I raise the question –

Is it just a dream, or is it the light untold?
Is it a reality that in dreams appears
And takes one on the trip to the heart of its own?
That brilliant burst in the light, could that be he?
Does he attempt in me his own light to espy
Wandering from God to the Outer Dominions?

As inside me, I seek the Outer Dominions,
Inside my dream, the Divine begins to unfold;
Before my eyes emerge the forms he does revive
With the ray from the depth of multiplication,
The bright source's birth is under my inspection,
Stream flowing into his seat of authority.
That is the world rousing from the heart of its own,
Through numerous rays, there flows the river untold
And at dawn, from the darkness, finally appears
And attempts with its rays the pathway to espy.
In the river, I bathe myself as I question –
Is it water or air, or is it perchance he?

"Water and the path and the air: all that is he,"
The water tells me with sparks of the Dominion.
By water and fire, the Cosmos multiplies;
It feeds the world with fire from the heart of its own.
Fire also asks me to restate the question,
If my fire is also real and untold,
Whether it destroys me or aids in revivals.
The heart's raging fire is under my inspection,
A rose from the very heart begins to appear
And bestows on the fledgling world authority;
Within the drops, the entire world is to unfold
Sailing up and down the stream of life to espy.

"Swim in the river and try a path to espy,"

He whispers instructing chants, and I hear from him:
"As you travel, let all your knowledge multiply,
Take wing toward the core in the home of your own;
On the road, you're under my closest inspection,
My path can offer you knowledge untold,
On my path, the light is all restored and revived,
On my path, you dream, and I ask all the questions,
My trail leads you straight to the light authority,
My path leads you to the gates of the Dominion,
On my path, everything emerges and unfolds,
On my path, the truth inevitably appears.

"In your dream, the truth inevitably appears;
It seeks deep within itself its truth to espy –
Within you is the place where the truth is revived;
Open up the door of the secret Dominion;
Only the truth can offer its authority."
I journey on, and I cannot help but question:
Is it in your darkness that lies the spark untold
That helps you to emerge from a dream of your own?
"Inside the spark, there is a secret that unfolds:
It spreads drops and rays and helps them to multiply, "
I hear him as, in the light, he whispers to me,
Traversing endless stretches under inspection.

In my dream, God's reality's on inspection
And I listen to the story where, it appears,
Both the cosmic dream and reality are he
And the dream and reality he multiplies
And inspires his dream in the world to unfold,
Tell reality with a dream world of his own.
What is real, and what are dreams? I question,
And he whispers back to me that dreams can revive
The waking world by which he gains authority,

And that, while dreaming, in reality, he 'spies
The name of God in the light of the Dominion
While the dream gives birth to reality untold.

Deceptions are the light of the truth that's untold.
In my light, I submit myself for inspection
In the light is where the dream ever does unfold;
I measure you with light and ask you a question –
Is it in the dream that the truth always appears
Flying on rays to the core of the Dominion
And relying on the rays, my dreams to revive
I rouse reality from the dream of my own
And in reality, to become what he
Is, who from the other side wants me to espy
And lift me to the light's seat of authority,
And with my dream, will his waking world multiply?

"Only through dreams does reality multiply;
Only in dreams can the reality untold
Be begotten and born out of the light," says he,
And inside the dream, he does make his truth appear,
Opens the path to the core of the Dominion.
All along the way, I'm puzzled by the question:
In what way, within the rays, his dream is revived
And in what way in a dream it ever unfolds,
And how it shines from the heart of authority
His dream that I, awake, submit to inspection,
And how come, like I, he too attempts to espy
A new light that suddenly shines on its own.

Why did he give me so much more of my own,
I know not. Why does he ceaselessly multiply?
Why tell me the secret of the Dominion?
In real reality, light's under inspection,

And in a real dream to me, he does appear;
In front of my eyes, there commences to unfold
The real dream from which he does whisper to me
That it is he who speaks from authority,
That he is the only reality untold,
That, when I wonder, he is my every question,
That when I seek, it is he who tries to espy
And as I dream, in his own dream, he is revived.

With the help of forms, he gets the whole world revived.
The stars raise him to his seat of authority,
From which, among the stars, he starts to multiply
Aiding the truth that the world needs to appear
By explaining what is a dream and who is he
That his own light in the world covets to espy;
While the truth of the dream is about to unfold,
Into the dark, he pours the spring of the Dominion.
Does he watch me, or is it all my inspection
Or does the dream bear a reality untold
And directs God toward the one throne of his own?
Even further, evermore, I walk and question.

Divine Ray has its own authority
To revive the rays that lose strength so he can ask
The biggest question and the truth untold
Hides in the rays that appear to multiply
Proof of Dominion. Under his inspection,
The ray starts to unfold – it looks for sky to espy.

III

To you, o Creator, now I pay a visit,
To you, the almighty Lord of all the darkness.
The light's your guest of honor, and in it, you bathe.
Turn me into a ray so I begin to see
You, as well as your face, in addition to your
Foundation, so I can see where the light is born.
Tell me now, reveal to me what it is that hides
In your unfathomable depths, as well as deep
At the bottom of the darkness in your bright heart.
Tell me, is there one and one only Overlord,
Or are you, perchance, the very Master of light?
Is the darkness really your father who conceals
His face whenever he is confronting your glow?
Please tell me now, do reveal to me your secret –
Are you your own father as well as your own son?
Is there anywhere in this dark any way out?
Is all of the secret contained in solitude,
In the struggle to overcome the powerful
Amount of the omnipresent and complete dark?
The Lord of Darkness is by far the most ancient
Witness of the birth of light and of every game;
The Lord of Darkness is the father of the ray,
And your son himself is the very light of day,
Born out of the emptiness and out of your dream.

"The origin of the secret lies in my dream.
Come into my dream while paying me a visit
To see the magnificence in the light of day
Being born from the heart of the ancient darkness
And how everything dives into the world of rays.
You are a ray in which you regularly bathe,
But you still do not know the secret of the game.

You hesitate and shy away; that, I can see.
I am the dark and the ray that's the most ancient,
From inside me, there also shines the heart of yours,
Whereas I shine from the heart of the ancient dark
That helps the world and you inside it to be born.
The light that shines out from my core is powerful;
At the bottom of its world, the whole world does hide
As it keeps daydreaming deep in its solitude,
The ray lingers in its heart, waiting somewhere deep,
Inside itself, it seeks a passage and way out.
The whole universe is concealed inside my heart;
That tiny-yet-enormous world is my own son;
He is the only life-affirming Overlord,
He readily wakes up and resolves the secret,
He is the source of all existing hope and light,
He awakens himself with rays of his own glow;
And the entire truth within him is concealed.

"The eons-old darkness inside him does conceal
Both the many sources and the light of his dream
That narrates the darkness with its innate glow.
Do come to me, pay me a sudden visit
So that I can tell you the secret of the light
As well as the origin of time and the day,
To take you to the very core of the secret,
In the very core of the world and the darkness,
To see therein the deeply dormant Overlord
And how the world slowly awakens from the ray,
So you can see who is my father and my son,
And so that you can dive into his ray and bathe
And find in the deepest recesses of his heart
The reason for, and source of, the world and the game,
So that within his heart, you may find a way out.
An exit you seek and anticipate, I see,

And the exit is not outside but hidden deep
By the darkness and the ray that's the most ancient;
It patiently awaits its light in solitude;
It awaits itself and the inquiry of yours,
While in the dark, from the reach of darkness, it hides.
And while the light slowly awakens from its dark,
Inside it, darkness is concealed and powerful.
It is the very force that to all rays gives birth,

"It is the one secret from which your world is born;
Deep within, the father and the son it conceals.
The blackest darkness is the light most powerful,
Hidden deep inside the heart of every dream
That lives far beyond the reach of the total dark
And subsists inside on the diet of the glow
Of the deepest dark that itself may ever hide.
It permits nobody to pay it a visit;
That is why you don't know the origin of yours
Sailing blindly toward the harbor of the light
And seeks along the way omens in solitude;
It seeks the sources of the original day,
It looks for that spark, the ray that's the most ancient,
To awaken and inspire the dormant secret,
To plunge into itself and reach the parts so deep,
To open up its eyes from within the darkness
And to exclaim at the top of its voice: 'I see!'
I'm truly the darkness and light's Overlord,
I am the passageway and the only way out;
All my springs issue forth and flow out of the ray;
All the extant galaxies are merely my games;
I am truly my own only father and son;
The entire world dreams of itself inside my heart;
In the expanse of its sumptuous light, you bathe.

"In the primordial cosmic fires, you bathe
As you observe a river that is being born
And springs up only to flow back into the heart,
Each conceivable secret inside it conceals;
You are not mistaken; what you see is his son:
An enormous cloud and a river powerful,
Born out of that particular amorous game
With the emptiness that awakes him from his dream
And sends him off on a long journey of the ray
From the deepest core of the primordial dark,
In a quest for the pathway, hope, and a way out,
To create himself with the help of innate glow
And to become the dark's exclusive Overlord,
So that from the darkness, at last, he'll cease to hide.
It is this very truth that you're seeking, I see;
That is why you're looking to arrange a visit –
You'd like to descend into the heart of darkness,
For that would instill peace into the heart of yours
And so that at the world's brink, out there in the deep
You could quench your thirst with its pure, essential light,
So that you could absorb his absolute secret,
And that in your bright and exquisite solitude
You would understand the source and home most ancient
And that is the birthplace of the light of your day."

There can be nothing more exquisite than your day:
In innumerable dominions, you bathe,
You are my day and my home that's the most ancient,
Inside you, the light of the entire world is born,
You dream of us, invested in your solitude,
You are hopeful to come across us in your heart;
It's because of us that you suppress a secret,
Inside you, an exquisite flower is concealed;
It sprouts straight out of the core of your innate light.

That luminous flower that grows there is your son,
And you dispatch him on a quest into the deep;
He is nourished by your truth that's most powerful,
And he grows from the soil that is the truth of yours,
Willing to partake in the omnipotent game
And springs out along with the light from the darkness,
He springs out of the most obscure depths of the dream
And greets the emptiness that is on a visit,
So that he would open up the space for the ray.
I see how you burst out and issue forth, I see,
I see your home gleaming spectrally from the dark;
And your face no longer has any need to hide;
Both for me and in yourself, you are a way out;
I see that you are now the only Overlord,
That the dark subsists on your own nourishing glow.

I swim in the river, and your inherent glow,
I observe the truth in the bright light of day.
You are the truth! the most powerful Overlord,
In the truth of light, you are immersed, and you bathe,
In light, there lies your strength as well as your way out,
You are light, and the home that is the most ancient,
Inside you, the power of the dark lies and hides,
Inside you, the vast expanse of the dark is born,
Your light can't possibly exist without the dark;
Without it, you'd wither away in solitude;
The dark is expanding inside you, that I see,
The dark gives birth to a flower inside your heart,
So that the world would spurt and fly out of the ray
And spread far and wide the most powerful secret;
It sprouts and grows when the dark comes to visit.
Your inside light will no longer remain concealed;
It bursts free and spreads all around out of your dream,
And all the innumerable angels of light

Spread filling the vast expanses of the darkness,
And thus, the darkness learns that you are her own son,
Born out of a tempestuous amorous game,
While still in its heart, in a place hidden and deep
The darkness preserves the glorious name of yours,
For she is your valley that is most powerful.

All your worlds and your strengths that are most powerful
Subsist on and respire your quintessential glow;
The heavens are nothing without the strength of yours,
Without the glorious azure light of your day
That penetrates itself far and reaches quite deep
And whispers to the darkness who's the Overlord,
Who's the one that lights and sends the sparks from this game
In which sparks you also immerse yourself and bathe,
You declare, "Than the father, greater is the son
For the Son offers salvation and a way out
Of the immortal and never-ending darkness.
You are a conqueror, God that's the most ancient,
You demolish darkness and emerge from the light.
Inside you, it expands; deep within you, it hides
It becomes a part of the game of your own dream;
The more it penetrates, the more children are born,
New worlds and dimensions inside, it conceals;
You awake them all in the middle of the dark,
And receive the vast dark that's come for a visit,
So that you would not disappear in solitude
And take to your grave your most closely kept secret.
A bud opens and evolves in the dark, I see
The one bud of the world, on the path of the ray,
Plunges down toward the deepest depths, to the heart.

The rose that lies dormant, undisturbed in your heart
Awakes like a celebration, all-powerful,

And deep inside itself, with the help of the ray,
It conquers the space with its never-waning glow.
All of the heavens, that is your face, now I see,
Swarms of stars, as well as all the angels of yours,
Whose flight helps you to illuminate the secret.
It is the world that is being born from your day
A family that's to counterbalance solitude.
Infinity dives and sinks into you so deep,
You greet infinity that's come for a visit,
Because you're infinity's mighty Overlord,
Because you are the light that counteracts the dark,
Because the world is constantly born from your game;
In you, the world's heart is permanently concealed,
In the innumerable worlds of yours, you bathe,
Inside them, your innermost light is being born.
The world is life, whereas life, in turn, is your son.
He is born and develops right out of your dream
And in a dream, he seeks self-escape, a way out,
Which the darkness within itself contains and hides.
You open up a path through the gates of darkness,
For without space, there can never be any light.
That's the path seeking the ray that's the most ancient.

Light up the darkness, you who are the most ancient
Ray: Attract the dark and pull it closer to your heart.
Your darkness persists and respires in the light:
The darkness of space is a depth most powerful;
Light cannot exist if devoid of your darkness.
The emptiness is the true birthplace of the ray,
The emptiness is the place where your life does hide,
You conquer it fully with a powerful glow
And using it, you cast out paths and a way out.
All of your luminous pathways now I can see,
All your expanse growing sparkly from the dream –

Flowers sprout and grow from the darkness of your light.
You are the supreme rebel but also a son,
You disclose unto the world the darkness's secret,
From your innermost desire, all light is born
And departs on the journey of the endless day.
In the totality of many worlds, you bathe,
The world helps you heal all your wounds in solitude,
In your inner expanses, our name is concealed;
And we are the path on the path toward the deep
Nucleus of your dream and flame-invested games.
You receive all the worlds that have come to visit,
You expand amid the endlessness of the dark,
You are light's and darkness's only Overlord.

The world governs a single Overlord:
You destroy the world's order that's the most ancient,
You're a river that has issued forth from the dark,
You conceal the whole universe inside your heart.
From the darkness, I come to you for a visit
So that I could quench my intense thirst with your light;
Teach me to partake in your mysterious games,
May I be guided by your hand all-powerful
Into your very heart's expanse that is so deep,
Where the universe shines from the heart of darkness
Where the truth in its entirety is concealed,
As is the spark of life of the almighty ray,
So that right by your side, in utmost solitude,
I could watch the daylight's ray in which a face hides,
And you submerged in it, as with the dark you bathe
And defend the ray by way of a pitch-black glow
While attempting to rouse it from the dormant day.
By embracing the dark, you look for a way out –
That is how, inside the dark, your world can be born
The dark finds a way out in you, as I can see,

It descends into every corner and secret;
You receive it at the deepest depth of your dream
To impregnate your ray and help a son be born
From the radiating core of the love of yours.

All the light is the product of the dream of yours;
It will become your true and only Overlord;
The expansive firmament is your only son.
He is the dissent, the ray that's the most ancient,
He lies dormant deep inside the heart of your dream
Awaiting to arise and emerge from the dark,
Into the emptiness, he whispers the secret
That is fast asleep inside your dolorous heart.
It surges up from the dream; that much I can see,
Receiving the dark that's come to pay a visit,
And the dark inside helps light to be born,
The dark glowing steadily from within the light.
In the darkness, light is looking for a way out
And can be heard singing from the luminous game,
Singing the truth of your dream and your holy day,
Diffusing throughout the darkness, all-powerful
Feeding the dolorous emptiness with the glow.
You remain inside the heart, somewhere very deep,
In the radiant core, you eternally bathe
Waiting for the son at the end of the darkness.
Inside you, the everlasting magnet does hide,
Inside you, the son's entire path is concealed,
You're awaiting him, sheltered by your solitude,
Watching him not stray from the path inside the ray.

Your prayer relies on the pathway of the ray;
The defiant ray's the path of the thought of yours
That radiates brightly from the dark solitude;
Without a bright world, you are a sad Overlord.

Light amounts to nothing if it is all concealed;
You are rescued from your dark only by your son.
The secret of the world inside himself he hides,
He breaks the dark order that is the most ancient,
With the light, he sinks into the heart of darkness,
And he rouses you from your perfectly calm dream;
In his ray, you are submerged, and with it you bathe
Whereas you peer into the distance from the dark;
You send out the spark from the heart into the deep,
So that it can unlock and release your secret
And bring you back to life with the help of the glow
So that you will no longer grieve inside your heart.
You are nourished by his fire, all-powerful.
Your illuminated face is what I can see,
Donned in a beaming smile in the bright light of day;
In your paradise, I'm to pay you a visit
As you offer me the keys to your secret game,
From which your every thought is begotten and born
That is your only world and your only way out.
The whole world is nothing but the thought of your light,

Just as reason is only a matter of light,
And all the matter is but the thought of the ray,
A thought compressed into matter is the way out.
Those luminous rays are only the thoughts of yours
Your omnipotent knowledge aids them to be born,
You sum up the whole world in your bright solitude,
You set the thoughts on fire as a part of your game;
You are the entire thinking world's true Overlord.
That is the reason you approve of my visit,
So that I could read the memory that conceals
The truth of thoughts, as well as the truth of the day,
From whose tempestuous gales your son's to be born.
His brilliant, beaming face is what I can see;

Inside of you, he no longer wishes to hide,
But sends into the world a thought, all-powerful
As well as the ray that's truly the most ancient
So that it would not wither enclosed in your heart.
A flower sprouts from emptiness and darkness,
To warm the darkness with its omnipotent glow,
And you nourish it with the waters of your dream;
Whereas along the way, it decodes its secret
In his rebellion, you are submerged and bathe.
All the stars out there that are diving in so deep
Are the tears of joy from the expanse of the dark.

The world is the joy of the newly-awake dark;
It takes flight on the wings of thought out of the light;
Nourishment of the most ancient darkness so deep
It provides with the thoughts of your wandering ray,
With which you, submerged in the emptiness, do bathe
And out of the darkness, discover a way out,
And throughout the heavens, you diffuse your secret
From the spacious heart of the very thought of yours.
Enormous world issues forth straight from your dream;
Through the glimmering sparkles of thought, light is born;
Concepts and ideas that are quenched with the glow
And nourished with care in the divine solitude,
Within the rays, they issue forth from the darkness
And embark on the glorious path of the game,
With the sole purpose of returning to your heart
For you are indeed their only true Overlord.
You are their home primeval and the most ancient
In your void, you receive them on their every visit,
To construct a structure towering, powerful;
It is inside them that your knowledge is concealed.
The light of your thought, a letter within does hide;
It writes it in the sky on the path of the day.

All your starry letters I can follow and see;
I read the book that's flying out from your son.

"The whole wide world, all of creation, is my son.
The world relies on fire when battling the dark.
You are in awe of fire, as far as I can see,
Knowing that the ray is the very thought of light,
Knowing I can never exist without a day,
Knowing that the secret's glow reaches inside deep
And that deep inside it is where thought chooses to hide;
It starts to diffuse around from within the ray,
In its frigid body, it keeps the son concealed.
Inside my own truth, you are submerged, and you bathe;
You are being guided by his hand powerful,
So that you could find in your darkness a way out
And to come to me on a prearranged visit
When, at my shrine, I'd confide in you the secret,
So that you may see the ray that's the most ancient,
That will fully illuminate the face of yours,
Making you thus into your own true Overlord,
Awakened by the rays coming out of my dream,
You will smell the whiff of the secret in my heart,
You will realize how a bright flower is born,
You, in light, will become a flower of its game,
Washed over by its sumptuously fragrant glow,
And you will finally leap out of the darkness,
Leaving the cold death behind in its solitude.

"You appear hopeful to find me in solitude,
You know that you, too, are my honorable son,
And so you beseech with the rays from the darkness
That I appear to you in the midst of the dark,
And bestow upon you the knowledge and its glow.
You seek to attain some of my light, as I see;

You'd like to join me in partaking in my games,
To follow me inside the pearls of starry light,
So that you could see how a pearl is made and born,
A pearl straight from the source of the very first day
Born inside the fertile expanses of my heart.
The pearly root extends and reaches darkness deep,
It sprouts right out of the core of the dormant dream,
And therein where the name of the secret ever hides,
Therein lies your dormant, eternal Overlord,
Therein, he sleeps dreaming of the paths of the ray,
Therein lies enshrouded the very name of yours,
Therein, every cosmic pearl is fully concealed.
That is the pearl of the dark that's the most ancient;
In its distinct fragrance, you are submerged and bathe;
That is where you find the fully flourished secret;
You are conquered by its fragrances powerful,
On petals, it takes you to pay it a visit.
That flower petal is what offers a way out.

"In the heart of the flower, you find a way out,
You find a passageway burrowed through solitude.
The bloom-covered passage leads you to your visit.
And you are a son, just as this is my own son,
This is my own sanctum, immensely powerful,
Therein, I dream-fashion all children from the darkness,
Therein from the darkness, I conceal the secret,
Therein, I'm darker even than the darkest dark,
Therein, before your birth, you are submerged and bathe,
Therein, you keep me warm with the help of your glow,
For I am your father, who is the most ancient.
The light that you shine is immensely bright, I see,
The darkness withdraws before you – and it conceals
Its face from all those flame-infested, scorching games.
My son's eyes are now looking deeply into yours:

Without your eye, there'd never be a speck of light.
My son was born out of the everlasting ray
So that your sight, too, could eventually be born.
My son rules the airspace as its true Overlord
And without your eye, there could never be my day.
His power is inside you, and therein it hides
The power that nourishes the light in the heart.
Through your eyes, it observes from deep within your dream,
And serves you from the incomprehensible deep."

That is the sun that's sleeping somewhere far and deep,
From the eternal dungeon, it seeks a way out
To finally emerge with a ray of the dream
To prepare for life in absolute solitude,
And discover a passageway inside its heart.
The void flies through the heart, paying it a visit
Landing to bear and persuade him not to hide
But soar into the world, as he's the only son,
And obtain his vision from within the bleak day
Where so long there lay hidden the truth powerful;
To summon aptly the heavenly Overlord
Followed by fiery songs from the heart of darkness,
So that with every step, another ray is born
And he could write 'cross the world the sublime secret,
Which has blossomed with daylight out of the dark ray,
To give birth to a dimension from the darkness,
For without emptiness, there can be no light.
In the very emptiness, you're submerged and bathe,
The emptiness nourishes every step of yours –
Descend into the emptiness fed by the glow.
Therein lies the dormant secret of his own game
Therein lies for good the day that's the most ancient,
There, in the dark, the father has his son concealed.
The heaven of your primeval flower, I see:

A bud at the bottom of the atom, I see,
You preserve it inside your heart's bottomless deep,
Within it, both life and salvation are concealed;
There also lie your dormant hope and your way out,
And the eldest son awaits his day most ancient,
So that the gentle breeze coming out of the dream
Could beget him with the emptiness from your game
And employ it to make a stand for solitude.
The emptiness respires with the help of your glow,
It instills with hope the bud that is in the heart
To spread all around the dominion of yours.
You receive the emptiness here on a visit;
You wash your radiant face with it, and you bathe
In its inner regions, the space of the bud hides,
Throughout its vast expanse, there diffuses your light,
It is the manna to your all-powerful son.
It sinks into itself, to the heart of darkness,
Only to burst out into the light of your day
And holler using all of the might of its ray,
And to see the mighty bird's wings spread powerful,
To compose a song on your deepest dark secret,
And so that there may appear the bright Overlord,
To inspire new radiant worlds to be born
And to sing a song from the core of the darkness.

Roused by the emptiness, the bud of the darkness
Paces down the pathway of life, as I can see.
On its journey, the light diffuses and is born,
It plunges far to the core of the heart so deep,
To give the father's crown to the new Overlord,
To rekindle the light of the truth that conceals
At the bottom of the void, an ancient secret,
And search the dark void thoroughly for a way out.
There awakens the light of the bud powerful,

There awakens your universe the most ancient,
There awakens the life of your terrible ray;
It penetrates the world from the colossal dream,
Writing clearly in the sky the name of the day,
Giving birth to islands for the sake of the game,
Countless oases in the expanse of the dark,
To luminous signs counteracting solitude.
His mortal coil is spread all around by your son,
Who is nourished by your breath, sustained by your glow,
He extends in all directions the paths of light.
All the blood of the pathways strives toward the heart
In which the total power of the secret hides –
That is the driving force behind the spark of yours,
In which you are completely restored, and you bathe,
Where you receive me when I come to a visit.

"The entire universe comes to a visit;
It comes flying to me from the stormy darkness.
Therein, on your perennial journey, you bathe.
You arrive in the darkness by the ray, I see,
So that your soft, light-suffused, beaming face of yours
Shall appear to me in the germ where you are born –
Inside the ray, my nest gives you a place to hide.
You sail the light, backtracking right into the deep;
And you carry my heart along inside your heart;
You are all of my sons' true supreme Overlord,
For you are the sacrosanct edifice of light
In which the entire firmament is concealed.
Your heavenly roof is brilliantly aglow,
It writes out the entire perennial dream –
The love out of which my son was conceived and born.
You are my salvation, while I am your way out.
I am your shield from the darkness in solitude.
You are my desire, and I am your power;

You are my light, while I am the thought of the dark;
You are my youth, whereas I am the most ancient
Ray births you with the dark as part of the game;
You are the outcome of the dark's fight with the ray.
Inside you, the darkness spreads right out of the day –
And all my light starts to blossom out of the secret."

I have come to you now, in the germ of the secret,
On these wings to land here as part of my visit,
Carried by the wings of a radiating day,
Through the boundless vacant space of the darkness,
To arrange the meeting of two primeval rays.
I see you immersed in the spring in which you bathe:
The waterfall in the back is out of your game;
The world flows into the heart smoothly, I can see,
Returning to your home that is the most ancient,
Into the delicate nest of the thought of yours.
Once it grows weary of the unoccupied dark,
Your thought induces it once more to be reborn.
Your thought, a truth that is grand and most powerful,
The spirit of the matter source inside itself it conceals;
It gives birth to it from the thought in solitude.
Gold and silver lie dormant and still somewhere deep,
The atoms and the stars are seeking a way out,
The world gives birth to the thought inside of your heart.
The one who dethrones you is none but your own son,
Who thus becomes an all-powerful Overlord
Who is to spread your intellectual dream.
Innumerable thoughts develop in the light,
Nourishing you and your son with its inner glow;
Inside of them, your truth customarily hides

The origin of the day that appears to hide
In a sleep, awakes you from the depths of a dream.
It protects itself and you with a shielding glow.
In the light, it comes out to pay you a visit,
At the pearl-studded court of your essential light,
Into the spaces of your everlasting day,
Where light puts an end to every unsolved secret,
And where the world grows out of the heart of darkness,
Where you are the entire world's supreme Overlord,
Where the world is nothing but a thought of your ray,
Where you are the world, and the father, and the son.
In your profound, illuminating thought, you bathe,
The star-bound thoughts soar up and fly toward the heart,
Having glided straight out of your magical game,
To explore your heart on their quest for a way out.
And they go endlessly gliding through you, I see,
Going ever farther, plunging into the deep,
I can see them welcomed by the home most ancient.
The enormous world, created in solitude,
Returns once more into the tender nest of yours,
So that one more time therein, the world tries to conceal
From the overpowering expanse of the dark.
It's enticed to return by a force powerful;
The thought of the world that helps the world to be born.

You're the God, the darkness's dreaded Overlord;
On a secret journey, I come to a visit
To attempt to learn how your dark-begotten son
From the dormant inner glow ends up being born,
How you elevate him from the heart of the dream.
Your hope successfully hides him somewhere quite deep.
At the bottom of your core, I spot a way out,
I see you birthing him in fires played by the ray,
Bringing him into the world in the light of day.

That is the place where the most ancient bud you bathe.
Inside the bud, a powerful force is concealed
A game in the solitude by the love of yours.

IV

"Let me relate to you my entire story
About thought that conceives, gives birth to, matter,
About my matter predicated on thinking,
So you'd realize there is no duality,
That thoughts are my stars that perennially glow,
That through my thoughts there spreads a fragrant floral scent;
My thought observes from within the eye of the star.
All the elements constitute my memory:
As your biology is a reminiscence
That the path seeks as it's on the paths of knowledge;
My thought is matter that is in constant motion,
The endless world is the alert of the idea,

"All matter's nothing but the ray of my idea,
With the letters of atoms, it spreads the story;
From concept to void, the world exists in motion.
A single condensed spark's apt to conceal matter
That, while on the alert, issues forth from knowledge,
It slowly aggregates on the path of thinking,
As it spreads and sorts out its reminiscences.
Sound is the concept's speech; there's no duality;
There is nothing but outstanding memory.
All those enormous worlds that incessantly glow
Are my thoughts and my concepts that give birth to stars.
Through the emptiness, there diffuses my thought's scent:

"Through various senses, the world looks for my scent
Through them, it observes from the general idea;
Without flawless senses, there's no light from the stars.
Your ear is keen to hear the primeval story,
From within my mind, your eyes issue their glow.
My thought's on a long journey, always in motion,

To scatter all around the world my memory,
To fertilize the soulless and fallow matter,
To gift it the life of divine duality.
Substances are letters and digits of knowledge;
Substance is not matter but a reminiscence;
It imbues the void with the course of my thinking.

"That never-ending world diffuses from thinking;
It's your spirit detecting the multitude's scent,
It is the world recording my reminiscence,
As you grow and develop out of my idea,
You are the flower that grows out of my knowledge,
You are the fragrance of the effervescent star,
You're the fruit of unity, not duality.
Now lend me your ear; I will tell you my story:
If it weren't for the pain, you would not know matter
Or the real value of thoughts that are aglow;
Your guide across the world is my own memory,
In my thoughts, the world as a whole is in motion,

"Inside you, my concept is in constant motion,
My thought is present in your process of thinking;
The knowledge you have amassed is my memory.
That's the flower world of my thought-emitting scent,
The star-bound thoughts of my dreams are fully aglow,
Inside your own, you search for my reminiscence,
By the strength of your anguish, you measure matter,
By the force of poise – the might of my idea;
You proceed to narrate to me my new story;
I traverse the space on the wings of your knowledge,
For I'm you and you're me, there's no duality,
You are the inherent flame of the dormant star.

"Take flight toward the distances among the stars,

See, everywhere you look, something is in motion;
It's the life of my unity and duality.
Even gravity is inspired by thinking
That fly out of the very core of my knowledge."
Inside yourself, there awakens my memory
So that within you'd hear the story of my dream;
Your thoughts saturate my flower's scent.
All that you can see are only my ideas,
All those forms and shapes that are in the dark aglow.
Your mind listens to thought-oriented matter –
Within myself, you're born by my reminiscence.

"It's too grand a story of my duality;
All my hope relies on matter-inclined thinking;
Ideas issue forth from within my knowledge;
Within you, there spreads the scent of my memory.
On a long path, reminiscence's in motion,
So that in the pitch darkness, stars could be aglow."

V

Tell me about the heavenly flowers.
Such a vast world is your Elysium.
Please tell me about your innermost springs,
Embrace the melody of my prayer,
Tell me about your opulent gardens,
About your wondrous stark naked fairies,
And about your numerous winged angels.
How do you write down the music of dreams?
What musical symbols and what letters
Do you employ to compose the Cosmos?
Tell me the truth of your infinity.
How from the darkness do you raise the Sun?

"The whole darkness swallows the little Sun.
The countless rays are to all the flowers
Greetings from its sunlit infinity.
The dark's vastness is my Elysium
That aptly receives the fiery Cosmos
To be fertilized by the glowing springs.
The world flows out in watery letters,
Takes in the melody of your prayer;
Petals, fragrances – fly out of the dream,
And spread across the heavenly gardens;
The flowers converse with the angels;
And the angels make love with the fairies.

"I take pride and rejoice in my fairies;
It's because of them that I raise my Sun;
They keep company to all the angels,
They enjoy nothing more than the flowers,
They bask idly across all the gardens,
They grasp the murmur of infinity,

They are the most splendid pearls of the dream;
Their presence enlivens Elysium;
They take heed of all your earnest prayers,
They know all the words, all of the Cosmos.
Address them with the help of your letters,
Quench your thirst with the water from the springs

"That are fairy-like, and on those same springs
Start a conversation with the fairies,
Tell them all you know of the old letters,
And they'll tell you the birthplace of the Sun,
They will show you the entire Cosmos,
They will place you in the lap of angels
Who take heed of all your earnest prayers;
They'll show you the lasting court 'mid flowers,
And there and then, you'll see Elysium,
You will walk freely through all the gardens,
Entranced by the fragrant thoughts of the dream.
You'll open the door of infinity.

"And at the door of my infinity,
Worlds sprout, grow, and bloom from within the springs,
They plunge into the vast void from my dream,
Being intoxicated by fairies,
They spread light around across the gardens,
They fill the emptiness with their letters,
To spread the light through all Elysium,
To conjure up the light of my dear Sun,
To send food to my numerous flowers,
To spread fragrances throughout the Cosmos,
To hear out the letters of my prayers,
And go out into the world with angels.

"Converse outright with the star-bound angels,
Hear the sound of the lush infinity.
Those are the paths of your earnest prayers;
Your words fly hurriedly toward the springs,
They plunge into the dark depths of the Cosmos,
On their way through the void, toward my dream,
Their plea spreads the pollen of my flowers;
Your chant is endearing to my fairies;
Prayers in rays repay the tender Sun
That potently blazes in my gardens.
One of the prayers is Elysium
That I write out in luminous letters."

Your Sun awakens among the flowers;
At the very spring of all your prayers
Your name's written in letters from a dream;
It lands in the infinity's Cosmos –
An Elysium among the gardens,
Among all the fairies and the angels.

VI

Into the river, I plummet again and swim;
And from the river of your life, I do inquire:
Please do tell me now, o hidden Divinity,
Are you speaking to me, or is it just a dream?
To penetrate your secret is what I desire;
You who are my finest attempt at truthfulness.
Tell me what the world hides and its ability,
Reveal to me the secret of the firstborn day,
So I could see where your light commonly unwinds,
The resting place of the truth on starry display,
So I'd understand that the world's no nowhereness,
But a universe that's concealed inside your mind.

Inside of your very own, there's also my mind,
On the crest of your waves, I persistently swim
Right above your water is where the truth unwinds,
There is no way out of you for the nowhereness;
Submerged in your waters, I see you in my dream;
Escaping is beyond the world's ability;
For that reason, from deep within you, I inquire
To bring me forth and out into the light of day,
So I could see all your secrets, o Divinity,
As well as all your creatures on starry display.
All your river streams are imbued with truthfulness;
That is all I dream about and all I desire.

You know that it is your truth that I desire,
That the complete truth is contained inside the mind;
That my science is contained in your truthfulness.
You contemplate and yearn while I repose and dream.
Is there any achievement in our ability?
I wonder and ask you as through the gales I swim

And through the whirlpools, while with my will, I inquire
Of you to appear to me, o Divinity,
So I could see all kingdoms on starry display,
To see the place where your dormant bud now unwinds,
To see the persistent glow of the nowhereness
And its coming to life with the first light of day.

On every path, byroad, and highway of your day
The knowledge of the ray's origin I desire.
Tell me the full scope of the thought's ability
How expansive and breathtaking is truthfulness?
All your islands and reefs of hope I see in my dream;
The sprawling open sea with its depths is your mind,
Studded by luminous isles on starry display.
On my journey to your life, I pray and inquire.
You are my life, o luminous Divinity;
Your presence wards off the desolate nowhereness,
Toward your harbor, I sail on your ship and swim;
The harbor is the place in which the truth unwinds.

It follows you on end, with no time to unwind;
Your harbor's smile calmly radiates from the day;
You are my one light, as well as my truthfulness,
The truth of the whole wide world on starry display.
It is to you that I send prayers as I swim,
From the heart of darkness, I seek you and inquire.
You claim all's allowed and in my ability.
Are those your islands I keep seeing in my dreams?
Is it you that I find there, o Divinity?
Is this a mere confusion that's inside my mind,
Considering light is the one thing I desire,
To brighten up each corner of your nowhereness.

Through the expanses of the void, the nowhereness
Introduces space into the bud that unwinds;
In the void, there soars up and flies your truthfulness;
All the void-studded islands on starry display
Disperse and distribute evenly all my dreams.
For the light to shine stronger is what I require,
Traveling on end is the light's ability,
Support me on my journey as farther I swim,
Tempests and gales are raging on all through my mind.
Sometimes, even the day takes shelter from the day.
In the darkness of my day, it's you I desire –
Both darkness and light you are, o Divinity.

I address my prayer to you, Divinity,
Let me be heard now by the very nowhereness;
Without it, your path will lack the ability
To find a path; without it, there can't be your day
Nor a place that would inhabit the Devine mind,
Nor a sea to carry me along while I swim,
Nor the letters by way of which I inquire,
Nor your islands and your reefs on starry display
On my journey, could I e'er afford to desire.
The nowhereness is the shelter of truthfulness;
Therein, your primeval bud rests and unwinds;
I glide through it, observing you in all my dream.

Do I really live, or is it all a mere dream?
Tell me where the line is drawn, o Divinity,
Does the thought, even when it's wide awake, unwind?
Could there be deception even in truthfulness?
Please show me your face; that is all that I desire.
I've been hauled by this night and its starry display,
I imbibe the water and the rays as I swim;
Water whispers to me of its ability;

Engulfed in the ray, there's the radiating mind;
Within itself, it keeps the entrapped nowhereness,
Which is to receive all of the light of your day.
Tempestuous water seeks you as I inquire;

I am the water, sound, and ray as I inquire;
Submerged in your water, I see you in the dream;
All through it, I seek words and constantly desire
To find the meaning as I continue to swim.
Every drop flows toward you, o Divinity,
Every spark does pray to you only from the day,
Staying apart is beyond its ability.
Your letters soar up and fly on starry display,
Your light is never dormant and never unwinds.
The world's prayer is received by the nowhereness;
That prayer of the world is only your own mind
From which there issues the song of your truthfulness.

The life of the world is your very truthfulness;
With blest truthfulness, I pray to you and inquire:
Inside us, your dormant prayer fully unwinds,
Inside us, you pray to yourself, Divinity;
From within us, you issue forth into the day.
Your prayer's a vigilant presence while I swim,
It brings into view the water's ability,
It guides me firmly to the harbor I desire.
I observe all the islands in my starry mind;
Your thought studies mine as I inhabit the dream
It is all permeated by the nowhereness.
The greatest Sun of all is yours on display

Among other suns on majestic display;
The one harbor of your life is the truthfulness,
Smiling from the depths of the darkness and the day.

In the light and water, I see you as I dream.
Confide the secret to me, o Divinity,
And dance, for to dance with you is what I desire,
Don't allow your truth to fall asleep and unwind,
But help it shine like a bright star in your mind
Shining brighter is all that I require.
With ever-stronger strokes, I continue to swim;
All along the way, there resists the nowhereness,
But the dark divests it of its ability.

Blazing before the prayer's the ability
Of the shadowy nowhereness's deranged mind.
The whole world can be gleaned only through truthfulness.
There are no worlds beyond you, o Divinity,
In you, the power of the universe unwinds,
Your movement is absorbed by the stark nowhereness.
The fragrance of the rose's heart's what I desire,
For you are the rose of the radiating day.
I travel way too far in thoughts and every dream,
To your only bud, I pray, and I do inquire,
I glide above the islands on a starry display,
I discover the primeval rose as I swim.

I desire a blaze bursting forth from my mind
Lit by the light of day that inside me unwinds;
All abilities I observe, at times in dreams –
It's the World and truthfulness, o Divinity.
And I inquire no more, now I merely swim –
The whole nowhereness is now on starry display.

THE END OF THE DREAM OR MERELY ITS BEGINNING

- People equate religion with faith.

ARNAUT: Believing in God is faith, while prescribed religion is an act of mediation. Faith can survive without mediation, but religion cannot. Faith requires only God, while religion requires people to believe in even more than God. God is the incentive for creating a moral code. At the same time, in the case of faith, as a direct relationship with God, conscience, and faith, as internal regulators, become the strongest and the most effective code.

The truth remains distant, even though comprehending something that appears impossible is sometimes much easier. Its obviousness so blinds us that we seek causes beyond the world. However, the world is its own cause and consequence. Its own Father and Son. Its own God. The world is God. The fact that we don't know everything about the world is not that important because our role is to serve the purpose of the whole, not to encompass it. The fact that we cannot encompass the world and comprehend its origin does not imply that the world must have an outer cause or that it is without purpose and sense. That is the source of the greatest paradox, for it is often thought that there must be a cause beyond the world, while it is forgotten that the world does not need a cause. The world exists without a cause. It has always been there in all its various forms. The path and the division of the world conceal its life. A realized world is a dead world. That is why we don't need to know everything. Our greatest happiness lies in us not knowing everything.

- But we know some things, including that you and I are talking and that it is true.

ARNAUT: Don't be so sure. Perhaps you're only dreaming. We

feel and think, and that's what is most important.

- I wake up and realize that Arnaut deceived me in my dream by claiming he was alive. Perhaps he did not. Maybe I am only dreaming.

Notes on the form of particular poems

Ballad The second and fourth verses rhyme and are shorter than the other two, which do not rhyme. The language is colloquial. The following poems from Book One, the "Ballads" cycle, were written using this form:

"Unknown Heroes",

"The World and God",

"The Sumerians and the Nibirians",

"Lemuria and Atlantis"

Ballade (Ballata) It consists of three stanzas of eight lines each, which rhyme according to the following pattern: ababbcbC. The envoi: bcbC. The capital C indicates a verse that is repeated as a chorus. The same rhymes are used in each stanza in the same order. The poem "There is no day, there is no night" (Book One, the "Ballad" cycle) was written using this form.

Ballade Supreme It consists of three ten-verse stanzas. The rhyming pattern is ababbccdcD. The envoi: ccdcD, or – ccdccD. The D indicates a verse repeated as a refrain in each stanza. The poem "This world is the only truth" was written in this form (Book One, the "Ballads" cycle).

Burns stanza It is named after the Scottish national poet Robert Burns (1759—1796). The rhyming pattern: aaabab. The a-verses consist of four metrical feet, while the b-verses comprise two feet (in our case, eight syllables alternate with four). The poem "Shells and Snails" was written in this form (Book One, the "Old Source" cycle).

Domino rhyme The verses do not rhyme within four-line

stanzas, but each verse rhymes with a verse from another stanza. Verses two and three rhyme with the first and fourth of the next stanza, respectively. In the last stanza, the second and third verses rhyme, respectively, with the first and fourth verses of the first stanza. It was based on a troubadour song. The poems "The Way of the World" (Book One, the "Old Source" cycle) and "Nowhereness Inside Nowhereness" (Book Two, cycle "Nowhereness in the World") were written in this form.

Chant Royal A variant of the ballad. This French poetic form usually consists of five or three 11-verse stanzas and an envoi, or a tornada, consisting of five or seven verses. The same rhymes are used in all stanzas: ababccddefE; the stanzas may have anywhere between 8 and 16 verses; the envoi (tornada): ddedE. (Although 13-verse stanzas are not used in this book, here is the pattern for them: ababccddeefeG.) The poem "Our Dreams" (Book One, "The Old Source" cycle) was written in this form.

Rubai In each stanza, consisting of four lines each, lines 1, 2, and 3 rhyme. The poems – "The Third Eye" and "The Eye of Consciousness" were written in this form (Book One, "The Old Source" cycle).

Sestina The sestina was invented by the Occitan (Provençal) troubadour Arnaut Daniel (full name *Arnaut Daniel de Riberac*), who lived in the twelfth century. There are no rhymes in it, instead of which six keywords are used. A sestina consists of 39 verses – six stanzas with six verses each and an envoi, or a tornada consisting of three verses. Each verse in each stanza ends with one of the keywords. The tornada contains two keywords in each verse, one of which must be at the end of the line.

The pattern:

stanza 1: 1 2 3 4 5 6

stanza 2: 6 1 5 2 4 3

stanza 3: 3 6 4 1 2 5

stanza 4: 5 3 2 6 1 4

stanza 5: 4 5 1 3 6 2

stanza 6: 2 4 6 5 3 1

Various variants may be employed in a tornada: (1, 2 / 3, 4 / 5, 6);

(1, 4 / 2, 5 / 3, 6); (2, 5 / 4, 3 / 6, 1); (6, 5 / 2, 4 / 3, 1).

The following poems have been written in this form: "Chaos," "Love," "Hatred," "Love and Hatred," " The Secret," "The Reason," and "The Secret and the Reason" (Book Two).

Sestinas were written by both Dante and Petrarch (nine, one of which is double). Philip Sidney wrote the first sestina in English, and the form was used by Rudyard Kipling, Ezra Pound, Wystan Hugh Auden, Elizabeth Bishop, and others.

Rhymed sestina English poet Swinburne *(Algernon Charles Swinburne, 1837–1909)* was responsible for this sestina and the double rhyming sestina. In this sestina, keywords 1, 3, and 5 rhyme, as do words 2, 4, and 6. The pattern: ababab. The poems "The Surface" and "The Depth" (Book Two) were written in this form.

The pattern:

stanza 1: 1 2 3 4 5 6

stanza 2: 6 1 4 3 2 5

stanza 3: 5 6 1 4 3 2

stanza 4: 2 5 6 1 4 3

stanza 5: 3 2 1 6 5 4

stanza 6: 4 3 2 5 6 1

tornada: 1, 4 / 2, 3 / 5, 6

Double sestina in six stanzas These are the first sestinas of this kind. (They are represented under numbers IV and V in Book Two.) This sestina consists of 78 verses – six stanzas consisting of twelve verses each and a six-verse envoi.

The pattern:

stanza 1: 1 2 3 4 5 6 7 8 9 10 11 12

stanza 2: 12 1 11 2 10 3 9 4 8 5 7 6

stanza 3: 6 12 7 1 5 11 8 2 4 10 9 3

stanza 4: 3 6 9 12 10 7 4 1 2 5 8 11

stanza 5: 11 3 8 6 5 9 2 12 1 10 4 7

stanza 6: 7 11 4 3 10 8 1 6 12 5 2 9

tornada: 1, 4 / 2, 3 / 10, 12 / 6, 8 / 9, 11 / 5, 7 (sestina IV) and

12, 1 / 3, 4 / 9, 8 / 11, 10 / 2, 5 / 6, 7 (sestina V)

Double rhymed sestina The only such sestina so far was "The Complaint of Lisa," written by Swinburne. This variant consists of twelve stanzas with twelve verses and twelve keywords. The rhyming pairs are (1, 4) (2, 5) (3, 7) (6, 11) (8, 10) (9, 12). This book contains three such sestinas under the numbers I, II, and VI ("The Possibility of Cognition", Book Two). This sestina consists of 150 verses – twelve stanzas with twelve verses each and an envoi with six.

The pattern:

stanza 1: 1 2 3 4 5 6 7 8 9 10 11 12

stanza 2: 12 1 9 11 4 7 2 8 3 10 6 5

stanza 3: 5 12 6 4 7 1 2 3 10 9 11 8

stanza 4: 8 5 7 6 4 12 10 2 3 11 1 9

stanza 5: 9 8 6 10 1 2 7 4 3 12 5 11

stanza 6: 11 9 6 10 4 2 7 1 12 8 5 3

stanza 7: 3 11 7 8 12 1 2 10 5 6 9 4

stanza 8: 4 3 9 6 5 10 1 7 12 11 8 2

stanza 9: 2 4 5 1 3 8 7 10 9 11 12 6

stanza 10: 6 2 9 3 8 1 7 5 12 4 11 10

stanza 11: 10 6 8 4 3 5 9 12 2 1 11 7

stanza 12: 7 12 6 3 9 11 5 8 4 2 10 1

tornada: 12, 10 / 8, 9 / 7, 4 / 3, 6 / 2, 1 / 11, 5   (This is the arrangement in Swinburne's version.)

Various variants are used in this book with minor modifications.

The tornada of the sestina I: 12, 10 / 9, 8 / 7, 4 / 3, 6 / 2, 1 / 5, 11

The tornada of the sestina II: 12, 10 / 9, 8 / 7, 4 / 3, 6 / 2, 1 / 5, 11

The tornada of the sestina VI: 5, 12 / 8, 9 / 7, 4 / 3, 6 / 2, 1 / 11, 10

Quatro sestina It has 588 verses – 24 stanzas with 24 verses each and an envoi with twelve. This is the first sestina of its kind. (It is represented under number III in Book Two.)

The pattern:

stanza 1: 1 2 3 4 5 6 7 8 9 10 11 12 13 14 15 16 17 18 19 20 21 22 23 24

stanza 2: 24 1 23 2 22 3 21 4 20 5 19 6 18 7 17 8 16 9 15 10 14 11 13 12

stanza 3: 12 24 13 1 11 23 14 2 10 22 15 3 9 21 16 4 8 20 17 5 7 19 18 6

stanza 4: 6 12 18 24 19 13 7 1 5 11 17 23 20 14 8 2 4 10 16 22 21 15 9 3

stanza 5: 3 6 9 12 15 18 21 24 22 19 16 13 10 7 4 1 2 5 8 11 14 17 20 23

stanza 6: 23 3 20 6 17 9 14 12 11 15 8 18 5 21 2 24 1 22 4 19 7 16 10 13

stanza 7: 13 23 10 3 16 20 7 6 19 17 4 9 22 14 1 12 24 11 2 15 21 8 5 18

stanza 8: 18 13 5 23 8 10 21 3 15 16 2 20 11 7 24 6 12 19 1 17 14 4 22 9

stanza 9: 9 18 22 13 4 5 14 23 17 8 1 10 19 21 12 3 6 15 24 16 7 2 11 20

stanza 10: 20 9 11 18 2 22 7 13 16 4 24 5 15 14 6 23 3 17 12 8 21 1 19 10

216

stanza 11: 10 20 19 9 1 11 21 18 8 2 12 22 17 7 3 13 23 16 6 4 14 24 15 5

stanza 12: 5 10 15 20 24 19 14 9 4 1 6 11 16 21 23 18 13 8 3 2 7 12 17 22

stanza 13: 22 5 17 10 12 15 7 20 2 24 3 19 8 14 13 9 18 4 23 1 21 6 16 11

stanza 14: 11 22 16 5 6 17 21 10 1 12 23 15 4 7 18 20 9 2 13 24 14 3 8 19

stanza 15: 19 11 8 22 3 16 14 5 24 6 13 17 2 21 9 10 20 1 18 12 7 23 4 15

stanza 16: 15 19 4 11 23 8 7 22 12 3 18 16 1 14 20 5 10 24 9 6 21 13 2 17

stanza 17: 17 15 2 19 13 4 21 11 6 23 9 8 24 7 10 22 5 12 20 3 14 18 1 16

stanza 18: 16 17 1 15 18 2 14 19 3 13 20 4 12 21 5 11 22 6 10 23 7 9 24 8

stanza 19: 8 16 24 17 9 1 7 15 23 18 10 2 6 14 22 19 11 3 5 13 21 20 12 4

stanza 20: 4 8 12 16 20 24 21 17 13 9 5 1 3 7 11 15 19 23 22 18 14 10 6 2

stanza 21: 2 4 6 8 10 12 14 16 18 20 22 24 23 21 19 17 15 13 11 9 7 5 3 1

stanza 22: 1 2 3 4 5 6 7 8 9 10 11 12 13 24 15 16 17 18 19 20 21 22 23 14

stanza 23: 14 1 23 2 22 3 21 4 20 5 19 6 18 12 17 8 16 9 15 10 24 11 13 7

stanza 24: 7 24 13 1 11 23 14 2 10 22 15 3 9 21 16 4 8 20 17 5 12
19 18 6

tornada: 2, 10 / 14, 1 / 19, 15 / 13, 6 / 9, 24 / 7, 8 / 5, 16 / 4, 22 / 11,
23 / 20, 3 / 18, 12 / 21, 17

Sonnet corona   In the sonnet corona, the last verse of each
sonnet is the same as the first verse of the next, and the last verse
of the last sonnet is the same as the first verse of the first, thus
closing the circle ("Corona," Book One, the "Corona" cycle).

Terzanelle corona (Terzanelle)   A terzanelle is a modified
villanelle. Like the villanelle, it consists of five triplets and a
quatrain. The middle verse of the first stanza becomes the third
verse of the next, and so on; and in the last, sixth stanza, the
middle verse from the previous stanza is repeated as the third, and
the first and third verses of the first stanza as the second and
fourth.

Although this form has been used before, it is rarely pointed out
that its creator is the American poet Lewis Turco (1934,
"Terzanelle in Thunderweather"). Turco wrote his first Terzanelle
in 1965 and several more later. He is one of the main
representatives of the new formalism in America.

The terzanelle in this book (Book One, the "Terza Corona"
cycle – "The Awakening of the Day", "A Conversation Between
Darkness and Light") are located within the coronas in a series of
six terzanelles. The corona is structured in such a way that each
middle verse (despite often being modified) from the first five
stanzas of the first terzanelle is repeated as the first in the next
terzanelle (the middle verse from the first stanza of the first
terzanelle is repeated as the first verse of the second terzanelle, and
so on). The last stanza of the last terzanelle differs somewhat from
the others because the first and third verses of the first stanza are

repeated as the first and second of the last to allow the first verse of the first terzanelle to close the circle as the last verse of the last stanza in the corona, and for the third verse to be repeated the middle verse from the previous one, as in all the others.

In the corona "A Conversation Between Darkness and Light," under number 2, in the fourth stanza, the second verse – "On the path of light, I'm your watchful guard" – was not repeated as the third in the next stanza, but a new verse was created – "In my dark, dreams of your day I record." Also, under number 4, in the fourth stanza, the second verse – "From its own light the darkness radiates"– was transformed into "Dark flows into light-streams and dissipates" in the next stanza. In these two cases, the rule has been deviated from because, in this way, the third verse of the next stanza enriches the second verse of the previous one.

These are the first terza coronas ever created.

Terza rima (modified) The original terza rhyme that Dante used first in the *Divine Comedy* has this scheme: A-B-A, B-C-B, C-D-C, D-E-D and so on. In the poem "The Day in the Middle of the Path," Book One, the "Old Source" cycle, this pattern was not used, and there are only two rhymes alternating (which is more difficult, but this is only one poem): A-B-A, B-A-B, A-B-A, B-A-B, A-B-A, B-A-B, and an A-A couplet at the end.

Troubaduric song The same rhymes are employed in all the stanzas. All the first verses rhyme with one other, and all the second verses rhyme with one other, and so on. These are so-called external rhymes, with no rhymes within the same stanza. The poem "A Day of the Year" was written in this form (Book One, the "Old Source" cycle). Of the modern poets, Silvia Plath tried her hand at this form ("Black Rook in Rainy Weather").

Chaucerian roundel [*Geoffrey Chaucer,* c. 1343–1400]) It is named after Chaucer, who invented it based on numerous kindred examples. The first verse is a refrain repeated at the end of the second and third stanzas. The pattern: Abb; abA; abbA. The capital A indicates repeated verses. The poem "The Old Source" (Book One, the "Old Source" cycle) was written in this form.

Chaucer is the father of modern English literature and was the first to introduce vernacular English instead of Latin into literature.

Notes on the Creation Dates of Particular Poems

"The First Dream," "The Second Dream," and "The Third Dream" (the beginning and the end of Book One and the beginning of Book Two), were written in the early 1990s.

The poem "Nothing Has Ever Happened" from Book One was written in 2000.

Book Two (except for the prose part and "The Third Dream") was written in 2007.

The rest of the book was written in 2008.

The Index of Poems' Titles

The Index of First Lines

Far and wide, it is prey that hatred seeks,
Hunter has not beasts but himself to catch,
Nobody has gone anywhere,
We can't exist one without the other,
Transforming these words into purest light,
From Moscow to Berlin and Washington,
I plunge into the river again and I swim,
I pray that you open, O divine gates,
Is there a possibility of cognition,
The whole world breaks open before my eyes,
I tell you about my birth,
Rekindle the old source's flame,
Darkness and light have a conversation,
Down the river, through the whirls, I swim and question,
Tell me the secret as I look for you in dreams,
Words are what I choose to help me endure,
All that's hard-earned is genuine pleasure,
The world glimmers, the path does quake,
In our dreams, the world expands,
All your strength is deliberately small,
Your thoughts dive straight into the emptiness,
Trouble shows paths to those with open mind,
You realize that I am your homeland,
A sudden flash appeared inside my mind,
Inside the small sky,
On a calm eve, without the moon in sight,
The night hides the secret of chimeras,
Splendor lies in brave partaking in strife,
Hopeful, I sprightly go into the day,
The modern time is almost as strange,
All shellfish possess such weird frames.

ABOUT THE AUTHOR

Dejan Stojanović was born in Peć in 1959. He graduated from the Law School of the University of Priština. He has published books of poems:

Circling (Krugovanje), Narodna knjiga – Alfa, Belgrade, three editions – 1993, 1998, and 2000.

The Sun Observes Itself (Sunce sebe gleda), NIP Književna reč, Belgrade, 1999.

The Sign and Its Children (Znak i njegova deca), Prosveta, Belgrade, 2000.

The Creator (Tvoritelj), Narodna knjiga, Belgrade, 2000.

The Shape (Oblik), Gramatik, Podgorica, 2000.

The Dance of Time (Ples vremena), Konras, Belgrade, 2007.

Pentalogy: *The World in Nowherness (Svet u nigdini):*

1. *Ozar (Ozar),* Udruženje književnika Srbije, Belgrade, 2017.

2. *The World and God (Svet i Bog),* Udruženje književnika Srbije, Belgrade, 2017.

3. *The World in Nowhereness (Svet u nigdini),* Udruženje književnika Srbije, 2017.

4. *The World and Humans (Svet i ljudi),* Udruženje književnika Srbije, Belgrade, 2017.

5. *The Home of Light (Dom svetlosti).* Udruženje knjižcvnika Srbije, Belgrade, 2017.

The Hidden Light (Skrivena svetlost), Čigoja, Belgrade, 2018.

Primordial Spark (Iskra iskona), Albatros plus, Belgrade, 2021.

Centuries and Steps (Vekovi i koraci), Albatros plus, Belgrade, 2023.

Essays:

Creator and Creating (Stvaralac i stvaranje), Albatros plus, Belgrade, 2021.

The New Man and the New World (Novočovek i novosvet), Rad, Belgrade, 2022.

Anthology: *Selected Serbian Plays* (*Izabrane srpske drame*), USA, 2016.

Philosophy: *Absolute*, New Avenue Books, USA, 2024.

A book of his selected interviews, Conversations, was published in 1999 by NIP Književna reč, Belgrade. The Serbian Heritage Foundation and the Association of Writers of Serbia for Intellectual Engagement awarded the book the Rastko Petrović Prize.